SNOWBIRD'S
BLOOD

ALSO BY JOE L. HENSLEY

Robak's Run
Fort's Law
Color Him Guilty
Robak's Fire
Robak's Cross
Outcasts
Minor Murders
A Killing in Gold
Rivertown Risk
Song of Corpus Juris
The Poison Summer
Legislative Body
Deliver Us to Evil
The Color of Hate
Grim City
Robak's Witch
Robak in Black

WITH GUY M. TOWNSEND

Loose Coins

SNOWBIRD'S
BLOOD

JOE L. HENSLEY

St. Martin's Minotaur ❧ New York

This is a work of fiction. All of the characters, organizations, and events portrayed in this novel are either products of the author's imagination or are used fictitiously.

www.minotaurbooks.com

Library of Congress Cataloging-in-Publications Data

Hensley, Joe L., 1926–2007.
    Snowbird's blood / Joe L. Hensley.—1st ed.
        p.   cm.
    ISBN-13: 978-0-312-24111-7
    ISBN-10: 0-312-24111-9
    1. Missing persons—Fiction.   2. Terminally ill—Fiction.   3. Husband and wife—Fiction.   4. Older people—Fiction.   5. Florida—Fiction.
    I. Title.

    PS3558.E55 S66 2008
    813'.54—dc22

                                                              2007046628

First Edition: February 2008

10   9   8   7   6   5   4   3   2   1

Dedicated to
Harlan Ellison from his friend and pal, Honest Joe.

Also for
Missie and Bob Suggett
Sister Marie Emery
Babe Matthews
Kendra and Maurice Auxier
Wilma and Tom Champion
Gay and Tony Hertz
and of course
Kathy and Mike

SNOWBIRD'S
BLOOD

-1-

Tourist

C annert happened upon the auto court after the better part of a day of driving. The motel, that being what it was now called, was far off the interstates on a secondary Florida state road. It wasn't greatly different from other remodeled auto court motels he'd seen except this one seemed more valiantly kept up and appeared as if it might have been recently repainted.

Martha's only card had come from Lake City, less than two hundred miles away. Cannert knew she liked two-lane roads and clean, cheap, small motels.

Besides, he had a hunch about what he now was seeing, and he'd learned during his sometimes dangerous lifetime to follow and believe in his hunches.

He turned off the car radio and unfolded a Florida state map from the cluttered glove compartment of the Ford. He was fairly close to Jacksonville, but still in Florida, well within half a day's driving range of Lake City.

Beyond the motel, Cannert could both see and smell the Atlantic Ocean. Here, the main body of the ocean lay east of a thin, likely unpopulated barrier island that protected the land. That island made interior land less valuable because land that lay on the ocean was worth far more than bay land.

Not many tourists likely came to this area. It was too far north, too deserted, and in winter too damned cold.

Tourists went where other tourists went. They looked for warm rather than cold.

The motel was a long, low building. When he got closer, he could see signs of age. It was, however, white roofed and not unattractive, the kind of quaint place that might have drawn his wife, Martha.

Cannert counted the units. There were twenty-eight. The unit setup had once been separate, closely bunched cabins. Now they were joined together by clever carpentry.

There was a black on white sign at the entrance: MOM'S MOTEL. SINGLES $35, DOUBLES $44. Below, in smaller letters: *Low Weekly Fishing Rates.* A small neon Vacancy sign also glowed dimly.

Cannert thought his vanished Martha would likely have noticed the sign if she'd passed this way. She had gone on to Florida to scout for a couples' retirement spot a month ago while he still lay in the hospital. Cannert now knew it had been a mistake to let her drive to Florida without him. He also believed, on bad days, that she was dead, but sometimes he awoke in the mornings and sensed her alive and lost out there in the fog and smoke.

He believed, at those times, that she was alive, and he remained in love with her.

It also seemed possible she'd left him, given him up as a futile job, but he didn't believe it except in the blackest hours of the nights when nothing was certain.

He remembered Vietnam and the black-clad men who'd come up from their underground hideouts and killed some of his army buddies and the hill people he'd lived among. When the black clads had gone back underground, he'd followed or awaited them and killed many of them, executing every damned one he could catch with gun and mostly knife.

He'd done similar things with other bad men after he came back from Nam.

He was following that pattern now in looking for his Martha. He would hurt no one except those who might have hurt her and those who schemed to hurt him or injure the good world he believed in.

That available list for harm was well populated in Florida.

He parked the Ford in front of the office unit and slowly got out. He liked watchers to think he was less than he was.

From the bay side of the motel there came a sharp fish smell. White gulls wheeled and flashed in the sun.

Two people, a man and a woman, watched him as he entered the office. The man put down his newspaper and Cannert saw the familiar headlines he'd first read yesterday in Jacksonville. Two days ago and miles away, near Live Oak, an unknown, likely demented (according to the newspaper stories) rifleman had conducted target practice on the office of a motel about the size of this one, killing one motel worker and badly wounding another. Cannert supposed that had made many motel managers extra watchful.

That headline had influenced changes in Cannert's travel style because of the cautions, although he'd not been the shooter. He'd changed his check-in approach to that of an itinerant, dedicated fisherman looking for a cheap place to stay while he pursued the wily Florida fish and perhaps played a few holes of golf. He'd discarded both his rifle and shotgun into the waters of a lake. Anyone who searched his car or suitcases would find nothing suspicious but might discover things of value.

"Could I see a room?" he inquired in his best courteous and gentle voice.

The man nodded, relaxing a bit. He was a big, fleshy man, not yet old but no longer young. He was much larger than Cannert, who was visibly aging but still looked wiry.

"You sure can, sir. You'll find our place clean and respectable even if it does have a few years on it. And we have a motel pool if you like to swim." His voice still had traces of the snow of New England in it.

The woman went back to the paperback mystery novel she'd been reading, hiding herself behind its lurid cover. Her eyes had shrewdly estimated Cannert and his possible worth and turned away, unimpressed.

Cannert followed the big man down a well-weeded walk. Like some heavy men, the motel man's step was light as a ballet dancer's.

The room Cannert was shown was old but acceptable. Sunlight came through a clean window. The bedspread was faded but immaculate. The towels in the bath were thinning but still serviceable. There was a quiet window air conditioner.

Cannert nodded his approval and followed the fat man back to the office. "I'd like to stay a week if it can be worked out. Maybe longer if the fishing around here's as good as I've heard."

"Try the big pier five miles south. It's called Citadel Beach," the motel man advised amiably. He shrugged. "It's just off the highway and can't be missed. I'm not a fisherman, but I hear others brag on the fishing on that pier."

Cannert looked out the office window. Only a few other cars were parked in front of the joined units, and it was late in the day.

"Looks as if business isn't so good today."

The motel man gave him a penetrating glance. "We make do all right. Times are hard in this part of north Florida, but things hopefully will improve. Most vacationers stay along the interstates or the beach roads farther south, but running this place is a tad better than welfare, and north Florida's climate is easy on our bones what with lots of sweet sun. Took Em and me almost five years to get the damned Maine cold out of our bones." He shook his head and grinned determinedly. "We'll never go back, never give up our place in the warm sun."

"Is your pool salt or fresh?"

"Salt." He appraised Cannert with care. "How about two hundred dollars for a week?"

"Done, and for at least one week." Cannert took out a worn

billfold and paid, letting the motel man get a glimpse of the thick sheaf of currency inside.

Cannert had hoped for a registration book so he could check for Martha's name, but he was handed a card instead. He filled it out and signed it "William T. Jones." The man behind the desk inspected the card and raised his eyebrows a fraction.

"Sure are a lot of Jones boys in this hard old world," he said, not smiling.

Cannert nodded. "The *T* stands for Thurman. The kind of Jones boy you need to watch out for is one who checks in with a painted woman plus a bottle of liquor. I'm alone and will be—all week. The only thing I drink is a bit of Canadian on special occasions." He looked coldly around the spartan office. "Where's the closest and best place to eat?"

"There's a good restaurant near the pier at Citadel Beach." The motel man looked down at the card, and Cannert saw him then look out the office window to check the license plate number written on the card against the plate on the back of the Ford. Cannert smiled to himself. They were the same.

"Thanks," Cannert said shortly.

"Glad to have you staying with us, Mr. Jones," the motel man said appeasingly. He extended a heavy hand. "Name's Ed Bradford. The lady you saw earlier is my wife Emma. We been here eleven years now. Making do in lean times and still hanging on." His smile seemed innocuous.

Cannert smiled also and shook hands. "I understand about being cold. I'm out of Chicago. Retired from construction. There was nothing to do and no one left to keep me in Illinois, so I'm wandering around, doing whatever I want." He nodded. "Golf a little, fish a lot."

"My bet is you'll like the fishing hereabouts," Bradford said, "but there ain't a decent golf course for maybe thirty miles. Not enough business around here to pay for building one or supporting it after it was built. They cost big money to build and maintain." He went back to alertly watching the deserted road out front, a brooding planner of a man.

Cannert left the office. He unloaded his bags and golf clubs from the car, leaving only the fishing gear inside. He then drove to the edge of the small town a few miles away. It was now almost dark, too late to fish. He found the restaurant near the pier and suppered there. Fishing talk came from nearby booths, and he listened. He tipped the waitress the correct amount and played a role he knew well, being and remaining unnoticed.

When he departed, it was into a moonless night. He drove back to the motel. There was only one new tourist car parked in front of a unit. A few children splashed aimlessly in the dimly lit pool.

Five out of twenty-eight rented. Not good.

Cannert entered his room. He drew the shades and checked things over. Someone had carefully gone through his bags. Only a watchful man would have noticed. The plastic-encased roll of one-ounce gold Canadian Maple Leafs and Krugerrands he'd left balanced on one side of a bag was now tilted wrong. Some of his clothes had been carefully lifted, looked under, then smoothed back.

Cannert turned out the lights and undressed. He smiled in

the dark room. His hunch seemed correct and he felt Martha was close. Losing her had angered him and also firmed up his purpose for what was left of his time. Cannert was a man who believed not all of life would be joy and fun. The good times had come and gone, and he no longer expected their return. It was as if his war years had returned to take their place.

He'd had a gift in those war years, and he knew he still owned it.

He hurt some inside, so he took a pain pill and washed it down with a glass of warm, brackish tap water.

He slept. There were shadowy dreams during the night, but no nightmares. Once he came full awake and plotted against the rest of his time. He'd found that it was now easier to hate the world around him than it had been, easier to use that hate to plan what must happen.

He slept some more and dreamed for a thousandth time of the blood and the blackness inside the Nam tunnels and of using his knife again and again without mercy. Later he dreamed also of Chicago and of bad times there. He didn't regret either of those times.

He'd been a bit old for the Vietnam War and was many years older now. But he'd been good at soldiering.

An optimist is a man who sees a half-full glass, a pessimist is one who sees the same glass as half empty.

Cannert knew he was now a pessimist. He could feel his rage rise each day as he read newspaper pages. The world around him was *bad*. He believed now mostly in children, dogs, and the hope of finding his Martha.

One must cope with the badness. Yet, at the same time, he could not be unfair. Martha would not like that.

After sunrise, he drove again to the fishing pier. He ate scrambled eggs and toast in the restaurant and then fished the day away. He was an indifferent fisherman, but a tourist needed to fit into some recognizable mold. What he caught he threw back when he was certain he wasn't observed.

He skipped lunch, ate an early dinner, then drove back to the motel. Again, there were few tourist cars. Other areas of the crowded state of Florida might be busy and prosperous, but this one, as Ed Bradford had admitted, was not.

Cannert changed into his bathing trunks and walked to the pool. A few children frolicked in the water and were watched carefully by their parents. The world was full of molesters and abusers, and parents knew it.

His bathing trunks covered the scars of two old war wounds that had almost killed him but didn't cover another scar that soon would.

The weather was muggy. Cannert dipped a cautious toe into the pool and found the water was warm as blood.

Ed Bradford came outside the office and joined him, smiling his ingratiating smile.

"How's fishing?" he asked.

"Pretty good," Cannert said. "I caught some good ones, but I gave them away. Would you like some fish if I catch any tomorrow?"

Bradford nodded. "On one condition. This place will be dead by tomorrow night. Sundays always are and you'll likely be the only one left. I imagine we'll close the place down. You bring back some fish and Em will cook them for us. Catch no fish and we'll unfreeze some steak. Maybe we could even have a drink of some of my cupboard Canadian Club first?"

Cannert smiled. "That would be fine. You're kind to a cold country stranger."

"You seem a kindred spirit," Bradford said, still watching him. Cannert saw he'd noticed the red scar that ran down from upper belly to a hiding place with the others in the swim trunks.

"That looks like a bad one."

"Car wreck," Cannert lied. "Slid a car under a semi on the damned Chicago street ice. Lucky to be alive." It was, in truth, the place where they'd last opened him after trying the chemo and radiation treatments. They'd hastily sewed him shut and given him the terminal news. It's spread and six months to a year, sorry about that, Mr. Charlie Cannert.

So maybe spend the days left to you drowsing and waiting to die in the sun?

Cannert nodded to himself. Not without Martha.

In the morning, Cannert again left early. Only one tourist car remained.

He drove for about a mile, found a turnoff spot, and parked his Ford, hiding it behind a billboard. He walked back up the beach toward the motel. A few other walkers were also on the beach, most of them oldsters getting in their healthful walking. A crudely painted sign along the beach said SNOWBIRDS

WALK and had arrows pointing both ways. Cannert had seen and heard the phrase before. It was a derisive one adopted by Floridians to jokingly explain the odd habits of out-of-state visitors who walked or ran the beaches compulsively, trying hard to restore health during a vacation week or two by frenzied exercise.

Walk or run in the hot Florida sun and live a little longer.

From a vantage point behind a hummock of sand, he waited until the final tourist car had departed the motel. He continued to watch. In a while Ed Bradford and his wife exited. They put a sign in the office window and then drove off in a two-year-old well-polished Chevrolet.

Cannert waited until they were out of sight and then walked to the motel. The beach was now deserted because the temperature had climbed upward with the sun. He checked the guest rooms and the office as he walked, but there was no one left. The sign on the office door read GONE TO CHURCH. CLOSED ALL DAY AND NIGHT SUNDAY.

The office door was locked, but Cannert found a window he could open. Making sure he was unseen by any solitary beach walker, he entered and searched through the office. The safe was locked, but he had no interest in stealing money. He wanted, most of all, to see the registration cards of those who'd come before him, but his search failed to turn up anything interesting.

He did find several things. In the kitchen, hidden behind the salt and flour, was a medicine bottle half full of a colorless liquid. Cannert unscrewed the top and sniffed. The odor was unfamiliar, not acid, but instead heavily alkaloid. About two ounces of sluggish liquid was left. He was unsure about the contents but believed it possibly was an unmarked poison. He emptied the bottle into a toilet and flushed it away. He then washed the bottle carefully, making sure not to get anything from inside it on his hands. He found a bottle of clear Karo, sniffed it, and put two ounces or so of it into the bottle. The liquid Karo sloshed about in much the same fashion as the previous contents.

He put the revised bottle back in its hiding place and prowled some more. He found a .38-caliber Colt revolver in a drawer. It was old and had some rust, but was loaded with fresh-appearing ammunition. Cannert left the weapon loaded but knocked the firing pin off with a hammer he found in the office. He took the firing pin with him when he departed and dropped it in the deep sand near where he'd parked his car. He kicked sand over it.

The beach walk was deserted. The sun sent the heat straight down at a walker, hot enough now to burn the unwary.

The exercise of walking in the heat and the excitement of breaking and entering had tired Cannert so that he felt faint. He took a strong pill and rested. He got out his vial of sleeping pills and broke up a dozen of them. He took the remainder and put them in his shirt pocket, then ground the broken bits into fine powder with a coin. He put the resulting powder back into the vial. All the time he was doing the grinding, he kept watch from his hiding place. When he saw Ed and Emma go by in their bright Chevrolet, he waited until they passed. Then he pulled his Ford out and returned to the fishing pier.

He wondered if he'd figured out the possibilities they might have planned for him and believed he had. If not, life was a gamble he was already losing day by day.

Fishing was good at the pier. He caught three fat fish and hooked them on the stringer inside his bucket.

Once, during the afternoon when his stomach was quiet, he got a ham and cheese sandwich from the restaurant and drove again back to the pull-off place near the motel. He ate the sandwich and then walked the sand dunes back to his hummock so he could check things out again.

The sun was now a round ball of molten gold. The Bradford car was parked near the office. Out front the neon No Vacancy sign showed.

He saw nothing, but he sensed and therefore knew they were inside waiting for him.

He returned to his car and drove once more to the fishing pier. Other fishermen around him talked fine weather and fishing luck, but he ignored them and waited patiently for the afternoon to pass. When it came time to return to the motel, he filled the Ford with gas and also filled an emergency five-gallon can he kept in the trunk.

Martha, maybe I've found you.

The church sign had been removed from the office door when he returned, but the No Vacancy sign by the road still glowed. Cannert parked his car near the office and waved at Ed Bradford, who sat perspiring, wearing rumpled khaki pants beside the saltwater pool.

Emma came out, smiling, and Cannert reflected that it was

the first time he'd seen her smile. She took the fish he'd cleaned before he left the pier, nodded her approval, and vanished back into the building.

Ed Bradford pointed at a bottle of Canadian Club and a bucket of ice.

"Build yourself a Canadian," he ordered affably. "There's water for mix, or I can get you a 7-Up or a cola from the soft drink machine."

"Water's better."

"Sit here up close. Tell me more about yourself. Tell me just how cold it gets in damn Chicago and I'll compare it to damn icy Maine." Bradford smiled engagingly at both his Florida world and Cannert.

Cannert mixed a light drink and took a chair by the pool. He rambled for a time. It was a story he'd told before. Some of it was true. There was no one for him now, no wife, no child to speak of, no surviving brothers or sisters. He admitted to Bradford the truth about the red scar. He detailed the long, pain-filled treatments and said he was now waiting out the time to see if they'd stopped the alien thing that grew and spread itself inside.

This last tale was a lie. The answer was known.

They sipped their drinks companionably and watched the sun fall from the sky. Finally, Emma came out to the pool.

"Dinner in a few minutes," she said, smiling again at Cannert. "Do you drink coffee, Mr. Jones? I'm afraid I forgot to get tea last time at the market."

"Coffee's fine—black, sweet, and strong," Cannert said.

His answer brought a smile.

Bradford kept adding to Cannert's drink, but Cannert was careful to sip. He spilled liquid into the sand when Bradford wasn't watching, then added more water.

When the sun was almost down, they moved into the rooms behind the office. A kitchen table bore lighted candles. There was a festive bottle of wine.

"Let me open that for you," Cannert said jovially, seizing the opportunity. "Wine tastes better if it breathes a little."

He observed them smiling at each other. He took the wine bottle and corkscrew to a corner and managed to dump his vial of powdered pills into the wine.

"I love wine but can't drink it these days," he said. "It burns me." He held up his drink glass. "I would take one more light Canadian and water if you would be so kind."

Ed Bradford fixed him a fresh one. It was dark brown with whiskey, and Cannert fought and controlled his stomach when he sipped it. He excused himself, used the toilet, and poured half the drink away, replacing it with water from the bathroom tap.

They ate companionably. The Bradfords toasted their wineglasses with his tiny sips of Canadian.

"No business at all tonight?" Cannert asked with interest.

"Sometimes, on Sundays, I just shut her down. All I seem to get on Sundays are problems. Besides, it's church day for me and Em, a day we like to share with each other. And also it's God's day of rest."

The meal was Cannert's fish. Emma had doused them with lemon and then baked them. They were good. On the side there were individual crisp green salads and tiny potatoes.

"New potatoes," Emma boasted. "And the salad fixings are fresh. No canned stuff. Me and Ed like to eat good."

Cannert nodded approval. "You people know how to live, and I do appreciate your kindness to me." He watched sharply, but the food seemed to be served and shared haphazardly and so was not suspect.

Em brought him his coffee—hot, black, sugary, and strong. Cannert sipped it, then added sugar. The coffee already tasted strongly of syrup and the sugar made it sweeter, but he drank it.

"Tastes strong," he said appreciatively.

They nodded. Cannert could sense them waiting.

In a short while, he could see they were growing sleepy, and it was time.

"My wife vanished down here in Florida. I miss her a lot, way too much to just easily lose her," he said conversationally.

"A wife?" Ed asked. "I thought your wife was dead."

"No. She came down here to find a place for us when I was in the hospital. Maybe she might have stopped here? She'd have been traveling alone under the name of Martha Cannert. Large woman, but handsome, gray hair, driving a four-door blue Plymouth with lots of miles?"

"She might have stayed here, but I don't remember her. And I thought your name was Jones." Bradford stirred uneasily. He tried to rise but had problems. "What's wrong here?" he asked. "What's wrong with me, Em?"

"I put something in the wine," Cannert said softly to both of them.

The two of them looked dumbly at each other, almost ignoring Cannert.

Ed Bradford finally shook his head and made it ponderously to his feet. He staggered to the drawer that held the gun. He dug it out and aimed it in Cannert's direction. He closed one eye and clicked the gun twice.

"I knocked the firing pin off your revolver."

The motel man reversed the gun and came toward him, but Cannert, quick and cat agile, easily eluded him.

"It's only a sleeping powder," he told the two of them soothingly. "I need to find out about my Martha. I think she maybe stopped here and you got rid of her? That's what you had in mind for me, isn't it?"

"Still do," Ed Bradford muttered. "We'll wake up. You won't."

Cannert bent over, acting out inner pain. "Something inside does hurt bad."

"It's poison," Emma whispered triumphantly, her eyes gone yellow. "I put it in your coffee. A drop or two is all it takes to kill. You haven't got long left."

"And my Martha?" Cannert pleaded.

"Maybe we got her, too. We do people now and then. Maybe there was someone like her. We favor single travelers, but you can't always find just one alone when there's a need." Emma gave him a sleepy look that seemed apologetic. "We have to do it to survive, you know. We can't fail again. We can't go back up where it's cold and where we have relatives who believe we're well-off. Therefore we can't lose this place. We've got to make it work. Times are hard. So, now and then, we do someone or more than one. Someone like you. The Mister will pray over you nice after you're gone and we'll bury you down deep under the sand. We'll sell your car or call the junk man to get it. The Mister"—she nodded at her dozing husband—"knows about that. He used to be in the used car business up north."

"Martha wore half-glasses and liked bright clothes. Her Plymouth had Illinois plates." He thought for a moment. "It would have been a month or so ago."

Emma started to snore. Cannert moved quckly from her to Ed and shook him. The fat man's eyes opened.

"Did you and your wife kill my Martha?" he asked.

"We'll wake up," Bradford repeated. "You . . . won't."

Cannert alternately searched the office and tried to shake one of the Bradfords back to consciousness. The only result he obtained from either Bradford was moans and mumbles and threshings about.

He found nothing in the office to convince him Martha had been or not been a guest at Mom's Motel. He did find some guest cards in a file in the back of a drawer in the desk. He went through them. The cards had gaps in their consecutive numbers, and he theorized they'd destroyed the cards of those they'd killed. Going back two years, he figured eight missing numbers. Eight or more dead. None seemed to be dated close to the time Martha had disappeared.

In anger, he scattered the cards on the floor. He then destroyed his own card. He tore it to tiny bits and flushed it.

He eyed the sleepers. He could leave and it was pretty certain they'd say not a single word. But they'd soon kill again for new potatoes, fresh salad fixings, and, next year or the year thereafter, a brand-new Chevrolet to drive to Sunday church.

He waited until he'd not heard a single passing car on the road outside for a long time. He then loaded his car and drove it to the dark front of the office. He washed and toweled all the places he might have touched inside his own room or in the Bradfords' office and quarters.

Maybe someone would remember him, and the police would come looking. But there were tons of old men and women wandering the cities and roads in Florida. Besides, it seemed possible that police were already looking for him.

He went back into the office one final time. Ed Bradford now snored loudly, but Emma's breathing had grown shallow. He tried again to awaken them but without success.

He knelt and recited for them a well-remembered prayer from his boyhood, then another he remembered from his soldiering days in Vietnam, one that had been taught him by the holy man of the hill folks.

"Sorry," he said to the office walls. "Sleep you both well in hell."

He doused the office and the rooms back of it with the contents of the emergency can of gasoline he'd purchased earlier.

From outside the front door of the office he listened to the night and the road. Nothing coming.

He tossed in a match and dodged back from the sudden blast of heat and flame.

He drove to the highway. Behind him he could see fire already breaking out from under the eaves on the pool side of the office. There was a bright explosion as some windows popped out.

He drove slowly north and pulled off the road about a mile away. By the time he heard distant fire engines, the flames were crackling high in the sky. The motel had been old.

He started his car again and drove sedately on.

He reminded himself to read newspapers for a few days to see if there was any news about a suspicious motel fire. Even if there was no story, he'd lay quiet for a while. Newspapers and the careful reading of them were useful for his quiet times. The papers were full of both bad things that happened to good folks and stories about the bad people who caused those things.

Those bad people entered pleas of not guilty, made bond, and then, many times, did additional evil things. So did child molesters and abusers.

It was a filthy world. It also was the only world he had for the time he had left.

So he must occupy himself.

At a major crossroad he made his decison on which direction to drive.

He found a chain motel, slick, neoned, and air conditioned, near Jacksonville. Inside he took a pill and slept with only his dreams for company in the cold and antiseptic room. The nightmares came softly on this night, with known and unknown dead faces, a few Floridian, many North Vietnamese, plus a number of others. He tried without success to make the faces vanish. At the same time he liked seeing them. The holy man from the hill people had taught him how to live with vanished faces and even how to honor them.

In his dream, he touched them with his fingertip with its drop of blood as he'd been taught.

He awoke fully refreshed when it was morning.

2

Lost in a Funny House

At seven in the morning, Alma Dagley Jones, the ward attendant at Tepsicon Rest Hospital, would awaken Jane Doe and the rest of her women charges. She'd make certain all of them dressed adequately after using the clean but mossy shower and toilet room. She'd then lead the group to the cafeteria, where a spartan breakfast was served each morning to the institution's patients.

For a while it had been difficult for Alma to rouse Jane Doe, but that had now changed. Jane now was fully ambulatory and could also talk and understand well. She had no pressing medical problems and the only medications she took were the tranquilizers the state of Florida supplied in large quantities to its various state and private contract mental institutions.

Tepsicon was one of the latter-type institutions.

Sometimes Jane seemed completely normal, but Alma knew

she still had almost no real memory of what had happened to her before she arrived at the asylum.

The name she wore had been given her by Florida officials after she'd been found unclothed, lacerated, and battered and then dropped at an emergency room near a rest area. She'd suffered multiple knife wounds and a fractured skull. She'd early on been in critical condition. Police first theorized that a group of highway bandits had robbed and beaten her and stolen her car. Later they'd also thought it was possible that someone might just have dumped her after her assault when no abandoned car turned up in the immediate area. The police reports stated she'd been sexually abused both before and after she was assaulted. It described both old and new injuries, bruises that had faded to yellow, plus the fresher injuries of the last assault.

Someone had used Jane Doe badly. And, police decided, probably for several weeks or longer.

Captivity? It had happened before, but mostly it happened to young, stolen children. Pedophiles and abusers grew bolder in a society that sometimes willingly sold its young.

The police report concerning Jane Doe had been restricted so as not to alarm either the domestic and foreign tourist trade. No general news releases had ever been made. Attempts to check the woman's identity had come up empty. Jane's fingerprints could not be found in the files in either Tallahassee or Washington, D.C. There had been inquiries made about missing women, and the authorities did try to contact those who'd inquired, sending along photos of "Jane" plus a report about height, weight, scars, along with other such reports on other women.

None of the missing persons searchers had ever attempted to claim Jane, but several times a male person had called inquiring about someone who fit Jane's description. He'd wanted to know her exact whereabouts. Attempts to trace the calls had been successful on his third call, but the calling number was found to be a pay phone in a rest area.

No one ran the files of searches from earlier times, before Jane Doe had been found. There wasn't anyone assigned to do that job. And so she remained lost and unfound.

Ward attendant Alma believed that she and Jane Doe were of a similar age, late fifties to early sixties. Alma, who was fifty-nine, liked the way Jane carried herself, friendly, steady, in charge, and no nonsense. Jane was also a clean woman but not frilly. She wore the clothes the state supplied her with a touch of style, and she was handsome. Now and then Alma had noticed some of the security guards, particularly Odd John Dorwin, the captain, looking Jane over with interest.

Fresh nuthead meat.

On this morning Jane was already up and dressed. She was sitting on her narrow bed and clutching her almost empty purse. She mostly used it to carry her compact and her handkerchief.

"I pulled myself up and out of bed early," she said to Alma. She sniffed at the morning smells. Some windows behind her were open and a warm breeze brought in both the wet and dry flower and fruit scents of inland Florida. Florida was a land where things were either bursting into life or dying, and Jane Doe liked many of the smells of it.

"You're looking fine, honey. Your gray hair's real pretty this morning."

"I washed it last night. I sure like this weather," Jane answered. "I can smell the oranges growing."

Alma smiled.

Jane Doe knew Alma liked her. She tried to be friendly with all in her narrow hospital world, but she particularly liked Alma, who was black, bright, proud, and a first-class lady. Alma worked hard at her job and was kind to her charges. Some hospital attendants were lazy and mean to those under their control. So were some of the security guards and hospital maintenance workers. Hospital pay was low and workers usually stayed only until they could find better jobs.

Alma liked her job. She had family close by, lots of grandkids. And jobs were hard to find for older workers.

Once, when big Ginger Cotner, who suffered "spells" and couldn't always control her temper, tried to attack Alma, Jane had helped Alma hold Ginger until the guards could come and subdue her.

Alma had appreciated that a lot.

"After breakfast, can I go watch the road from the upper porch?" Jane asked, her voice low. She didn't like to ask favors and have other patients hear her.

"Sure. Sure you can do that, sweetie. But first I want you to eat a good breakfast so you can get all the rest of your strength back." Alma smiled. "You're loads better. You're stronger and now you understand how things around this place work real good. Do you realize that?"

Jane nodded in return and felt encouraged by Alma's words. Jane did know it, but there were still multitudes of unreachable spots in the darkness inside her head. Plus she was now beginning to be aware that people in her circumstances, people lost and unfound, could likely expect to spend their lives in the state of Florida institutions.

From an upper porch Jane knew she could look out over the scrubby trees, the hospital fence, and watch a Florida highway. She'd discovered the porch recently after she'd begun her restless daily walks, watching behind her all the time. No one was likely ever again going to be able to come up on her unawares.

In Tepsicon that meant mostly Odd John.

The porch fascinated her. She liked to go there and watch the automobiles driving up and down the two-lane road. People going somewhere, *anywhere*. Today she wanted, for reasons she couldn't fully fathom, to watch the road again.

When Alma told her it would be permitted, she lost her feeling of anxiety and became content to wait.

She walked along with Alma and others, no longer having to concentrate on putting one foot in front of the other. For a long time, when she'd tried to look inside herself for answers, there'd been nothing but blackness and empty holes. She could feel cold and heat, she could taste and smell things, but nothing inside or outside her body meant much to her. She could remember and say words, but at first the words were inappropriate and without meaning. She'd spent her first institutional days staring upward and outward, her eyes seeking the light, her mouth mumbling words. She'd walked during that time only if she was led or pushed.

After a while, the words had started to have meaning and things had become more and more clear. She'd learned to live within the hospital rules. She'd relearned walking, at first tentatively, now with confidence.

The scars had faded and the outer wounds healed. For a time doctors talked about a plate in her head, but the fractured skull had knitted well.

Most of the people who worked in the asylum weren't purposely unkind. There was, for example, an odd-looking, foreign, mumble-talking chief doctor who sometimes had her brought to his office where he talked to her. She couldn't understand all the things he said, but she did understand that no one, including the doctor, could predict whether she'd recover all or any of her lost memory.

For a while in the beginning there were men in police uniforms who came to ask questions that hurt inside her head when she tried concentrating on answers.

"Who? What and when?"

Her answers mostly were she didn't know and couldn't remember.

They early on asked her who might have made the inquiring telephone calls. The calls puzzled her also.

As time passed, tiny bits and pieces of memory did return inside. Such were things to think on and use to try to dredge up other lost memories.

She remembered now mostly being in the dark and being

held captive. She remembered that she had been hurt and molested many times. More than that, she remembered fear and anger because of rude body parts on and in her, multiple hands holding her down and touching her private areas.

"Old bag of shit. Screw her to death. Hit her again and make her screw harder."

No identifiable recalled faces, but many remembered angry voices. How many had there been?

A lot.

By the time those memories returned and might have been of some use, the uniformed men had forgotten her and stopped coming around. Her case had been dead-filed. The only questions remaining were those asked by Doctor Abdulla Kassan, who'd been born and mostly educated someplace where most men and women were dark complected, like Asia or Africa. Kassan was the chief doctor at Tepsicon Rest Hospital. Tepsicon was a contract mental hospital. The overrun of patients from the big state mental hospitals were sent to Tepsicon, patients who weren't truly dangerous to themselves or others but were so grievously disabled they couldn't fully care for themselves. Tepsicon ran cheaply, less expensive to operate for long-term care than the regular state mental hospitals.

It was a hospital without many visitors. There were rules that made and kept family visitation rare and uncomfortable. Most of the patients had no one close who any longer cared about them. Plus many of the wards were locked, occupied by patients who might be dangerous if crossed or angered and were kept under almost constant sedation.

Breakfast this day, for those who were able to appear, was fried doughnut halves, fresh orange juice, and lots of black coffee. Some days there were eggs, greasy fatback bacon, and burned or unburned toast.

Jane finished breakfast swiftly so that she could go watch her road. The road was interesting, and she was now certain that she'd once driven a car on roads like the blacktop two-lane state road outside the hospital. She could remember bits on how it was to drive, turning the key, putting the car in gear, turning the steering wheel, watching the road carefully. And there was someone sitting beside her.

Someone beside her?

She tried hard, sitting and thinking, but no other lost facts filtered through for now. It was only that she remembered that there'd once been a face. Male? Female?

Someone or some group of someones from the dangerous lands beyond the fence had once stolen away her car and then her clothes. She wondered if that one or group of someones might be the person or persons who'd called the authorities about her, trying to find where she was. Maybe he, *it was one man,* still sought her.

Later, she did sit on the porch. Alma had left her there and gone to other work, of which, she always said, "there was aplenty."

Jane sat beside Ginger Cotner.

Ginger mumbled now and then but said nothing intelligible to Jane. She drifted in and out of consciouness, her cooked brain ruined by several thousand bouts with alcohol and multiple drugs taken orally or smoked or injected. Sometimes she was suddenly and mercilessly violent, but not often and not on this day. Ginger was a big woman, taller than Jane, eighty or ninety–plus pounds heavier, much of the extra weight pads of fat. Jane wasn't afraid of her.

The weather was warm, the sky lightly overcast, and Jane napped and awoke and then drowsed again.

Off to the side, Jane could see orange groves. Some of the groves were a part of the hospital, and sometimes patients who were willing and able were used to pick oranges. But today, for whatever reason, no one worked in the groves.

Cars appeared on the road for Jane to see, sometimes singly, sometimes two or more at one time.

She watched the cars, trying to see something that might jog her memory. After a time she found that the cars she was trying to watch were all driven by males.

She decided it must have been a man beside her when she drove the car that had been taken away from her. Or maybe it had been a man who'd taken her car.

"Hello out there," she called out softly to the cars.

Ginger Cotner, asleep on a nearby chair, never stirred at the sound of her voice.

Odd John Dorwin came past once and looked out at them. Jane thought he might have come out to pester her if she'd been alone, but when he saw there were two women on the porch, he moved on.

She hated the security captain. He'd pinched, patted, and prodded her. Once, after her strength and reason had returned, she'd caught him unawares when he'd tried to pat her on the belly. She'd left him gasping in pain with a hard, quick fist to the testicles. He'd hit her back, but he was more careful now. And also, she thought, perhaps more interested.

She let herself fall farther into uneasy sleep in her wicker chair beside the comatose Ginger Cotner. The constant tranquilizer drugs made day sleeping easy.

In her dream that day, a faceless male mob tore at her clothes and pulled them from her. There was pain, great pain. She remembered pushing bodies away and then losing the battle when the ill-smelling men of various ages came at her again. She also vaguely remembered cooking food for quarrelsome men at a camp in a woods where the men worked cutting wood. That had gone on for a while. She remembered sounds, screaming, fighting, motorcycle and auto motors, then a deep darkness that lasted and lasted for the rest of the forever until she'd awakened from a dark place at Tepsicon.

One special man in the mob had either hated or loved her. She believed that the one special man had either ordered her death or, more likely, saved her. Was he insane?

She still lived.

Spaced here and there in the dream, she remembered better things. There was also a good man somewhere outside in the fog of gray, someone faceless, someone who'd once needed her badly and perhaps still did. And she had been joined to that man for a very long time. And he was sane.

Remembering old love brought her up from the dreaming.

She came fully awake. The sky had clouded over and a thin rain spit tiny drops into the trees and the road. She sat under a roof, but still the warm rain affected her, making her break into a sweat.

Ginger Cotner was gone.

It was past time to leave the porch, but still she waited and watched.

Along the outside of the fence she watched a solitary man seemingly patrol the outside grounds. She soon saw he was not a guard. He walked stolidly and not well in the rain, looking in toward the hospital buildings. She could not see him plainly and she believed he was, for now, unaware of her. He walked something liked lost patients did.

He soon moved out of view.

She surveyed the high fence that enclosed the hospital. It was old, built mostly of concrete and stones with lines of rusty wire, still somewhat secure.

There was a guard force. Sometimes patients tried to escape. Most failed, and those who didn't fail were usually soon caught. Still she believed a determined person could easily scale the fence and, if prepared and well planned, escape. And there might be easier ways to run away if she was trusted and allowed outside.

But escape to where? She'd not thought much on leaving until now. It was usually warm and comfortable and safe inside the mental hospital. There was enough food. There was even a kind of society in the ward and she knew she ranked near the top of it. There were enough women for a card game and women sane enough to talk with. There was Alma if she grew tired of games and the many times irrational conversations. Now and then the "safe" ward women were transported into the nearest town in an old hospital van. There, they were allowed to visit the library, and some retail stores allowed them in to shop.

The library books and magazines were fascinating. The last time she'd visited, a kind library assistant, witnessing her excitement, had shown her files of old daily newspapers. She wanted, next time, to spend her hours in the library reading those papers.

Safe and secure.

She was unsure about what it was that lay outside. Maybe it was bad, but it might also be good. Was it worth taking a chance?

She eyed the fence again. The wind had come up a little and some rain blew under the roof toward her.

Odd John Dorwin opened the door to the porch and started to come out, but she made a threatening fist, ducked under his arm, and escaped inside laughing at him. He was arthritic, old, and owned no residual quickness. She was far more agile than he was.

He frowned at her in chagrin but didn't pursue her.

And so it went.

Time moved on slowly.

The town library newspaper files were fascinating. She read mostly the daily papers from the nearest big city, Jacksonville. She read news stories of fighting and killing in Europe and Africa, Iraq, Iran, and Afghanistan and the Mideast. She read about crimes in the streets of America, a revolution or two or three in South America, and bombings all over. Something came into her head and she remembered she'd been involved in a bombing once. Had someone tried to bomb a place she lived in like they now did often in other countries?

Nothing clear came to her.

She perused pictures showing the before and after of the twin towers in New York City. That disaster seemed familiar to her.

There were also stories about fashions, fancies, and alternate lifestyles, stories about beautiful women and handsome men.

She found it interesting that near Orlando, a sniper roamed the overpasses and shot at motorists with deadly accuracy until police killed him. Someone also apparently set fire to a small coastal motel miles north of Jacksonville after drugging its owners. That had happened on a slow newsday and was prominently featured with photos of the burned buildings and the ocean behind them, plus photos of the two deceased owners, dead of both smoke inhalation and the fire.

Juveniles shot and killed each other and their parents and teachers, in and out of schools. Rapists, stalkers, and deviants sought and found prey. Men and women armed with high-powered pistols and rifles took vengeance on coworkers, strangers, friends, and families. Robbers robbed and burglars burglarized. Men with bombs, willing to die with their victims, victimized much of the world.

She found herself fascinated by the bad news. That world became familiar to her again, although she had not much personal memory or knowledge of it.

She liked the ads, especially those for clothing. Fleeting visions came to her concerning past events, vague memories of crowds in malls, stalled auto traffic, children smiling, and shining Christmas trees. She enjoyed those remembered visions, without being sure whether they were real and true.

But the crime news was what drew her most, the reports about the sour, dangerous world that lay beyond the safety of the Tepsicon fence.

Should she flee over and away from that fence and into that surrounding world of danger?

She looked over weather forecast pages, trying to find things that sparked her interest. There were major stories about earthquakes, hurricanes, and tornadoes and a huge tsunami that killed hundreds of thousands.

The northern city names seemed most familiar to her: Milwaukee, Indianapolis, St. Louis, Detroit, Chicago.

Chicago?

She read almost all, then began to skip most of the same old international news after a while.

It had, she thought, always been that way both in the world and also in this country, She realized with certainty what surrounded her was her country. People hated each other and always would. She had no idea why it was that way and doubted the people did either. People hated and killed themselves along with hated others.

Confusing.

If she was to escape the hospital, she would need money. She understood you could buy things with money, bus tickets, new clothes, food. She had only the dole, the few dollars that the hospital gave in state payments to patients for toothpaste, cosmetics, and treats that could be bought at a hospital counter and in the town where the library was located.

She knew, from listening to patient gossip, that there were ways to make money in the hospital, some of them legal, some not. Drugs of all kinds came into the hospital and there was brisk trade in them. Some of the women and men attendants and guards would pay for sex, although some, like Captain Odd John, usually took it forcibly and free, but with care. Drugs and sex could bring quick, big money.

She discarded those illegal avenues, knowing somehow they weren't for her.

Legally, she could work in the kitchen or cafeteria for small pay. A few patients did, but working there had to be approved by the medical staff and also by the ward attendant.

She could wash and sterilize trays and dishes and/or maybe help in the cooking and serving of the food. If you worked in the cafeteria, you lost your state dole, but you made three or four times that much for the work. And you probably ate better also.

She made her decision. "Alma, can you please help me? You know I'm better and I know I'm better, but there seems to be no one outside the hospital who's seeking me or likely to ever find and help me, no halfway house, no way to establish my true identity and complete the paperwork for a job of my own outside. I'm stuck here. I'm a cipher. I want to work. I'll do any work they give me in the hospital or cafeteria."

Alma smiled at her. "I was beginning to wonder if it was that time yet. Sure, I'll get it fixed for you."

"Thank you."

Alma contemplated her. "You watch out for that guard captain. He's going to get you one day."

Jane smiled. "He's already tried, Alma. Believe me, he's tried. All he got out of it was maybe half a rupture."

Alma nodded, pleased but still not convinced. "Also, the guards and the yard workers claim there's a bearded man who comes to the fence sometimes on a motorcycle and sometimes driving a car. He looks inside with binoculars and without them. You go walkin' the grounds, then you best be careful." She shook her head. "More crazies outside than inside these days. This guy may be a crazy himself."

"Sure. Maybe I saw that one once."

"When was that?"

"A few days ago from the porch."

"Watch out for him," Alma said, her voice serious. "He could be dangerous. It's bad to have to say that to someone inside, but it could be that way."

Jane lay awake at nights and planned.

There were other things she'd need besides money. She had no identity papers of her own. She had no birth certificate, no social security number, nothing to convince the world outside that she was a person and not just a cipher.

She thought on it for a time until an idea came about where she could get an identity, one where the true owner would never miss anything or complain.

After a few months' work she was more ready. She'd built

up a stash of almost three hundred dollars. She'd acquired, from the gift room, a small suitcase where she now kept some of her clothes. Almost all patients had a suitcase. If the case was small, then you could carry it instead of your purse on trips to town. She began to do that.

Alma had smiled when Jane had asked for a suitcase.

"You've nothing much to put in one."

Jane had smiled in return. "I know. But I've got a job now and maybe I'll soon have more stuff to own and carry. There'll be a library sale soon. They have one once a year. I want to buy me an atlas. I want to look at the world and know where the places I sometimes dream about are located."

Jane still went on all the town trips, reading papers and magazines, trying hard to find a possible way to survive outside the hospital, reading want ads in the newspapers over and over.

The winter weather in north Florida changed from warm to unseasonably cold. Some days, outside, there'd be rain, and once there was an unexpected and much admired by the inmates dusting of snow. One cold night, hospital employees and patients burned smudge pots and started up huge fans to save some of the orange crop. The sun hid for days behind dark clouds, and many of the women, native to Florida, whispered disagreeably about "northers."

Hidden now inside Jane's pillow, in a small hole sewn neatly back, Jane had Ginger Cotner's social security card plus an old expired Florida driver's license that she'd stolen from the woman. She'd obtained them when Ginger had come again to the porch. She'd taken Ginger's because she'd never seen Ginger open her purse to inspect its contents. Ginger had no interest in such things. Most of the other hospital ladies jealously guarded their papers, their claims to being a real person, but not Ginger Cotner.

She'd had Ginger's papers for a month and there'd been no hue and cry. She'd exhume them from the pillow when she ran away.

Jane had resolved to go, but still she lingered. She believed that if she escaped from the hospital or from one of the hospital outings with Alma in charge, such might affect Alma's job. Sometimes other employees had charge of the trips into town. Now and then the one in charge was Odd John, the arthritic security captain. That would happen again sometime, she hoped soon. Then she'd make her escape.

She still visited the porch when she could.

It was there she saw the bearded man again. Before his face and body had been shrouded by the rain, but this time she could see him clearly.

He was out along the road. He had a big pair of binoculars and she could see he was looking her way. Behind him there was a motorcycle on a kickstand, a huge hog of a motorcycle.

The man was large and appeared to be powerful. He had no discernible weapon, yet when she saw him, she knew she had seen him before, and that someone who resembled him had hurt her and made her afraid.

Her head ached and itched inside.

She thought perhaps he now looked for her in anger or desire. And he had found her.

From his place out beyond the fence, he waved, smiled, and then beckoned to her.

She retreated back inside and hid for the rest of the day in her ward.

It was now time to run.

3

Seeker

Cannert lay on a couch in his furnished apartment. Through the back window he could see the attached garage of Davisson's house. The garage door was up and the red pickup truck gone. Cannert had been too weak to follow, almost too weak even to care that Davisson had left.

He thought that the cancer might now be eating him up.

Cannert considered entering Davisson's house again if he ever felt better. A more thorough search might turn up something, but he'd found nothing before. He doubted anything had changed. Also, Davisson seemed wary as an old fox and might have detected his earlier entry. He could be watching and waiting for another invasion.

The local Centralia police had once jailed Davisson but had been unable to hold him because there was insufficient probable cause for any criminal charge. If the police had found nothing incriminating, then Cannert doubted his ability to turn up more in a completely illegal search.

Cannert waited for Davisson to return. He was, at the moment, more worried concerning his own situation than about what Davisson was out doing.

He called a doctor who lived and had his offices nearby. The doctor came and checked Cannert over with expert fingers.

"My name is Dr. Allen Palmer. I seldom make house calls," he said, smiling gently down at Cannert. "Doctors don't have to, not even in this backwater part of Florida, but you interested me. You call and plead nicely and so I do an examination and discover you are sick, but then you refuse to come to the hospital and be seen and examined further there. I asked myself why. You were close by and so I originally came to satisfy my curiosity about your need. You're suffering from cancer, but I think you very well know that. How long did your previous doctor give you?"

"A year at the most. That was several months ago."

The doctor nodded. "Maybe you'll have a bit more time than just a year. You're not swollen. I detect no radical changes. Now and again there are times along the cancer way when things remain about the same." He shook his head reprovingly. "I'm not promising it will be that way always, but maybe you're nauseous and sick because you're not eating right. People who know they are ill worry about themselves and sometimes fail to eat right. What have you eaten today?"

Cannert recited a short list.

The doctor shook his head again and scribbled out a prescription. "Get this filled and then take one of the pills I'm leaving if you need it for pain. The prescription's for more of the pain pills. Try to eat regular meals. Stay away from high-fat foods." He looked down sternly. "And come to my office or turn yourself in at the emergency room of the local hospital. It will make it easier for me to examine you and I'd like to do a few in-hospital tests." He searched through his case and also handed Cannert a brightly labeled bottle of large tablets. "These are nonprescription. Chew up one, or maybe two if one's not enough, and swallow it with half a glass of water when you feel nauseous. They're only flavored chalk, but I promise they'll help. You can buy more over the counter in any drugstore. Ask the pharmacist for the brand name that's on the bottle if the pills work good. Or try another brand if you like."

"Thanks, Doctor," Cannert said humbly. "I do appreciate you coming to see me. I hate to go to hospitals." He smiled grimly. "People die there."

When the doctor had gone, Cannert discovered he was able to get up. He felt weak and his stomach churned, but he could walk. The doctor's words had helped him feel better. He went to the tiny kitchen, got a half glass of water, and chewed up one of the big tablets. It tasted chalky and sweet. He sat down and rested. His heart slowed and in a while he felt stronger.

He drove to a drugstore and got his new pain prescription filled. He took another of the pain capsules, then ate a ham and cheese sandwich at the drugstore's old-fashioned lunch counter. By the time he was finished with the food, he felt almost well.

He listened to the chatter of a few ancients sitting around

him at the counter. Centralia was a panhandle town, not many miles inland from the Florida gulf, a few more miles than that south of the Alabama state line. It was cheaper to live in the Florida interior than on the coasts. The town of Centralia drew old people, mostly those who were trying to survive on only social security and sparse savings. They lived in trailers and double-wides, and Cannert had seen them playing par-three and miniature golf and shuffleboard in their communes as they waited for their ever-approaching dying time.

Cannert remembered a pillow he'd seen in a Centralia novelty store. It read: *Poop on the golden years.*

He thought Centralia was the kind of town where Martha might have come to take a look. She might have even been intrigued by it. Martha was an educated woman. She'd graduated from college while Cannert had never finished high school. He'd lived by his clever hands and his ability to understand both machinery and how people survived injury. In the Vietnam War and afterward, he'd lived by his quickness and ability to hear, smell, and see well in the dark. And by his savagery and learned knowledge of the human body.

Martha would have liked the tranquility of Centralia. She'd have thought it would be a good place for him. She'd also have liked the fact that you could live there cheaply. Martha had much common sense and she'd watched their pennies.

In the newspapers he'd perused intently during his Florida travels, Cannert had read news items about old people disappearing from Centralia. One of the stories had mentioned a Lieutenant Tom Ryan as being in charge of the missing persons investigations. Another news story had said that an Alfred

Davisson had been picked up for questioning, then later released uncharged.

Cannert had come and found an apartment within sight of Davisson's place. Now he kept watch on that suspect while his own sands ran.

Keeping busy.

At five in the afternoon, an improved Cannert walked into the Precinct Bar and Grill. It was across the street from the police station. He took a seat at the far end of the bar, ordered a Canadian Club and water, tipped adequately but not munificently. He then waited. He'd been in the place twice before, listening and biding his time. A few regulars gave him tentative nods of recognition. He nodded back and then disregarded them.

Ryan sat five seats away from him. Cannert ignored Ryan for the moment. Another bar regular, a red-nosed patrolman who didn't like Tom Ryan, had told Cannert about Ryan's problems. Drinking had allegedly cost him his wife and also probably any chance for further advancement as a police officer.

Six o'clock came and Cannert still sat patiently. Shifts changed. Much of the early bar crowd moved on, going home or switching to other bars. A few couples came in, took booths, and ordered drinks and dinner. Ryan remained. Cannert surveyed the new arrivals and watched Ryan. A bartender waited.

"See if I might buy Lieutenant Ryan a drink and speak to him for a minute," Cannert said to the hovering bartender.

Ryan looked down at the drink and then nodded thanks to the buyer.

Cannert walked over and took an adjoining barstool.

"I do a little freelancing for a chain of small northern newspapers. I'm down here on a three-week vacation and I read items about missing people. I thought what I read might make a story for one or more of my papers. How many people are missing?"

"No one's sure. I'd guess a dozen. Maybe more, maybe less. Old people flit in and out of their trailors, condos, and apartments like butterflies in heat. They've got relatives in Saint Augustine, friends down in Tampa, and they last lived permanent-like in Detroit or Chicago. Nursing homes claim some. Some die, their bodies are shipped off and get buried elsewhere. A few I think are missing probably aren't. Some I don't list as missing maybe are."

He sipped the drink Cannert had bought him. "I doubt I could or should give you any help. There was this one guy we watched and eventually picked up for questioning, but nothing came of it. His name is Alfred Davisson. He's a bughead. He was seen hanging out with a couple of old people who later went missing. Also he openly hates old people." Ryan smiled without humor. "When his lawyer got him out of jail, Davisson sued for false arrest. Later he sued both me and the town because we kept surveilling him. Our local politicians don't like lawsuits, or me for causing such a terrible problem. I got an order from the chief to stop. So I stopped and I've stayed stopped. Guys like Davisson should die hard, but I guess in Centralia's world it won't be happening."

"You think Davisson was maybe involved in the disappearances?"

Ryan shrugged. "Only maybe, just like you say. And that's strictly not for publication." He smiled. "Also, not for publication's his nickname." He smiled and lowered his voice. "Around town they call him Dog Food Davisson."

"Why?"

"He runs a dog food factory."

"Okay. You said he was a bughead. What's that mean? I promise not to quote you if you tell me not to. And no one can make me, as a journalist, tell what you say to me."

"It means he's wacky. His elevator don't go even near the top floor. Davisson reads the papers and listens to the television. He knows lots of old people are moving to this area of Florida, and he bad don't like it. It doesn't matter to him that Centralia is poor and needs new people and their business. Davisson wants building permits stopped—he wants no more trailer parks and no more damned old people moving in. He makes good money baking his dog biscuits and so he spends it filing lawsuits against anything and everything, school bonds, golf courses, zoning changes. He's a great lawsuit man." Ryan grimaced. "He ain't popular, but he has got a following. Most of them are other kooks with big hates and tiny minds."

"And he runs a dog food factory for a living?" Cannert asked, already knowing but wanting Ryan to continue talking.

"He works in a dog biscuit factory. He's head man, I heard. Like I said, some people call him Dog Food Davisson. It's rumored to be a good job. Likely better pay than mine. We searched where he works and we searched his home and found nothing." He looked up into the bar mirror. "That factory of his is something. They don't have more than half a dozen or so people working days out there. Everything's automated." He looked Cannert over in the mirror and shook his head. "You also kind of look like a bughead."

"How's that?"

"Worn-out, sick, and tired to death. I can smell a zealot a mile away. Your eyes look sick of this world. Did you maybe used to be a cop someplace?"

"No. I guess newspaper reporting's the same kind of pressure thing," Cannert said, not liking the detective's acuteness. This cop was smart. "I learned to hate lots of things doing my job, but now I'm just a retired guy prying into interesting things, looking for a story to maybe make extra money."

"Okay," Ryan said tolerantly, losing interest. He looked significantly down at his almost empty glass. "I had a hunch about Dog Food Davisson. I did a police officer's natural thing. I watched him and I had him picked up. I asked him questions after reading him his Miranda. I then got a warrant and searched his places. All he did was not answer my questions, ask for a lawyer, and laugh at me. Then he called his lawyers again and I got my ass sued. The city attorneys say it's nuisance stuff and won't stick, but the people I work for don't like nuisances." He turned full face to Cannert and tapped him on the arm. "So I don't like Davisson. But I ain't going to tackle him again." He tinkled his ice impatiently.

Cannert nodded assent to the hovering bartender. "Another scotch for the lieutenant."

Cannert learned from looking in the phone book that the dog biscuit factory was located off a road at the south edge of Centralia. He drove his middle-aged Ford out past it the next afternoon. The building sat behind a high barbed-wire fence. A uniformed guard stood at the front gate. Davisson's red pickup truck was one of a half dozen vehicles parked in a paved lot inside.

The building inside the fence was long, modern, and gray in color. The only windows Cannert could see were high up, near the top of the building. A bright painted sign on one side of the structure read BOWSER'S BONE FOOD—FOR DISTINGUISHED HUNGRY DOGS. A dog with a big smile, a monocle, and a top hat held the sign. Cute.

Cannert drove on past and used a pine tree–lined gravel road around the plant for most of the journey. On the far side of the building he could see a loading dock. Two men worked there, pushing cartons into trucks.

As Cannert watched from concealment behind trees, two fairly new trucks entered the grounds. The driver of the first truck got out, nodded a greeting to the men on the dock, and pressed a button on a shiny pole. A large metal cover lifted automatically up from the ground. The driver reentered his cab and backed up to the exposed opening. Stepping down once more, he removed chains and a tarpaulin from the vehicle's rear.

Cannert saw animal carcasses. Some of the carcasses were horses, some hogs, some cattle. The driver attached ropes and hooks to the carcasses. They were lifted from the truck and then maneuvered into the opening without ever touching the ground. When the first truck was unloaded, the second one was backed in. This time the cargo was grain. It was unloaded down a metal chute that the second driver had on his truck.

Davisson came outside and oversaw the operation from the loading dock. Cannert watched him through binoculars and felt the hair rise along the back of his neck while his heart beat faster. This could be the man who'd gotten his Martha. Cannert had a hunch it was so. Martha's last postcard had come from Lake City, not far away. The man's strong appearance made him easy for Cannert to hate. And he had a certain feeling inside that this man was a killer.

Davisson was brutally built, maybe late forties or early fifties. He was balding with all his remaining hair cut buzz short. His eyes were small and cruel, his movements swift and sure. He seemed a man completely in charge of his own world.

With a rifle and scope, from this vantage point, the man would be easy enough to take down if Cannert ever became certain he'd killed Martha. But there might be easier ways where Cannert could do the job up close.

Cannert stayed motionless and out of sight and observed throughout the long, hot afternoon. At five, the other men, including the gate guard, left and locked the gate behind them. Davisson remained. At almost six, Davisson came out, got in his pickup, and drove it to the gate. He unlocked the gate, drove through, then locked up again. Cannert watched him leave, but waited. In a while, the red pickup came back past the plant, slowed, then moved on after Davisson had taken a long, careful look around.

A wary man, Cannert thought again. *He believes the police will come again and he wants to know it when they do. Why?*

Cannert extracted his little Hy Hunter Derringer .38, bought in a pawnshop, from the Ford's glove compartment. It was loaded with the two vicious wad cutters he'd placed in the chambers.

He found he was now trembly and feeling ill. He chewed two of the big white tablets. They helped some, even without water.

He parked the car in a small jungle of trees and then walked back. Halfway along the fence, he found a place where rainstorms running off higher ground nearby had carved a depression. A stout man couldn't have squeezed under, but Cannert easily managed.

The doors along the loading dock were locked and so was the front entrance. The windows were too high to allow entrance. Cannert prowled on for a time, then remembered the deliveries of the afternoon.

He pressed the button on the pole and watched the cover lift slowly from the ground. He clambered down the rungs of a metal ladder into the interior of the exposed cavity. He stopped for a moment to let his eyes adjust to the semidarkness. They quickly did. On this subterranean level, an inner door opened off into an area beneath the building. He found a wall switch to open the door above him and then entered through that door. He could see well even in the near-black dimness.

There was the strong smell of animals mixed with feed grains. Cannert made his way along a corridor until he discovered a stairway. On the floor above it became lighter and cooler. He moved past complex machines and huge vats, some of them bubbling. Relays clicked on and off. Motors whirred softly. Cannert inspected all, taking his time, stepping carefully, wanting to leave no trace. He found a marked switch that closed where he'd entered and he used it. An outside camera showed the closing.

At the front of the building, he discovered what he decided was Davisson's office. It lay behind a sturdy but unlocked steel door. Inside there was an impressive array of panels, switches, complicated gauges, and red and green lights blinking at the bidding of a nearby computer.

In the dim light, Cannert found Davisson's desk and chair. Papers were piled in neat stacks about the desktop. When Cannert held them close to the red and green lights, he saw that all were business letters or order forms. He put them back where they had been, making sure their order remained the same.

The desk drawers were locked, but in the corner of a blotter there was a twenty-dollar bill. Cannert smiled. A casual thief would likely have taken the money and Davisson would have known that someone had been inside his office. Or maybe it was left as a gesture of contempt for the Centralia police should they come visiting again.

The office appeared to be a dead end. Cannert went to the exit door and turned to take a final look. In a corner, a heavy wooden armchair, worn and scarred, caught his eye. It was the room's only additional seating. Cannert checked it and discovered a small opening between the cushion and the seat bottom, a place where something could be wedged. An idea and a hunch came at the same time.

He took the small gun out of his pocket and pushed it into

the recess. It fit snugly, out of sight. The derringer was an old friend he'd carried before. He considered the situation carefully and finally decided to leave the gun there. If he was wrong about Davisson, losing the gun was a small price to pay. But if he was right, a hidden weapon could be valuable. Guns were cheap and readily available despite the many federal and state gun laws.

He left the plant as he'd entered. He opened the metal cover once more and then closed it behind him with the outside switch.

For nine days Cannert kept up his watch on the factory and on Davisson's house. Davisson's routine varied little. Early mornings he'd be off to the factory; in the evenings he returned back home. No side trips but constant watching behind, wanting to see if there was a follower. Cannert stayed close, turning away when he became afraid of alerting Davisson.

Several times, at Davisson's house, people visited, breaking the monotony. Once, some kind of meeting was held. A tall man dressed all in black gave a blessing to begin it. People got up and talked heatedly while Davisson sat without movement and/or nodded his agreement from a front table. At one point in the meeting, bumper stickers were passed out. Cannert later watched Davisson attach one to his truck. It read PANHANDLE FLORIDA FOR PANHANDLE FLORIDIANS—OTHERS DIE AWAY.

Cannert felt well again. His appetite had almost fully returned.

He did a few things about town. He visited the local library, read about Centralia and its citizens, good and bad. Mostly he maintained his vigil.

Finally one night he saw Davisson turn out his lights and leave the house carrying a package and wearing never before seen dark clothes.

Maybe hunting?

Cannert got to his own vehicle as quickly as he could, panting a little, short of breath. He waited until Davisson's truck exited his driveway. He followed as Davisson drove within the speed limit down the main highway in the direction of the dog biscuit factory.

Seizing an opportunity, Cannert passed the red truck, cutting Davisson off slightly. Hearing the pickup's horn blare angrily, Cannert raised a placating hand, wanting to be noticed.

When he was five or six hundred yards ahead, Cannert pulled off the road, turned off the ignition, and popped his hood release. He got out of the car quickly and stood looking down at his seemingly disabled car.

The truck's lights picked him up. Cannert knew Davisson was seeing Illinois plates and the body of an aging "outsider."

The red pickup sped on past. Cannert felt his heart slow as the gambit failed. Then, at the next crossroad, he saw brake lights come on. The truck made an illegal U-turn, then another, before it stopped behind Cannert's old Ford. Davisson got out.

"Problems, old timer?" the younger man asked, his voice gruff but polite.

"Guess my car's getting old, like me," Cannert responded ruefully. "I passed you and then it sputtered and quit. Fate, maybe. Could I get you to drop me at the nearest service station?"

"Sure," Davisson answered easily. He smiled, but the smile never touched his eyes. Davisson was even larger up close, very formidable.

Cannert climbed into the cab of the red truck.

"You're new around here, ain't you?" Davisson asked.

"Just moved to sunny Centralia a few weeks back. I've no relatives left up north. Right now I'm in an apartment, but I'm looking to find me a cheap trailer. I need medically to be in a climate like this. And it's cheaper here than farther south down along the Gulf. I guess I also like freshwater fishing better than salt."

Davisson nodded. Cannert saw him glance into his mirror. The road behind them was deserted. No followers, no witnesses.

Davisson said, "I have to make one stop first. I manage a factory that makes animal feed, mostly dog food. I need to do a quick check on the machines there. Sometimes we let them run all night."

"No complaint from me," Cannert answered, smiling. "A lot of you folks down here in Florida are kind to us strangers. Makes a man glad he came here." He sighed. "Somebody up there's still on my side, I guess. At least I hope so on days I feel half good."

He saw Davisson nod coldly in the half darkness.

"Yes, sir," Cannert added heartily. "That's sure the way of it."

———

At the plant, Davisson opened the gate, drove through, then got out and relocked the gate.

"Company regs," he explained. "Got to keep things locked up tight after dark."

He parked in front of the building. From the bed of the truck he got out his package and then came to Cannert's window.

"Come inside with me. Take a look. It's mostly dials, switches, and the like, but people say it's interesting. During the days I've a few men who help out here, but I could do most of it alone if I had to. Follow me and let me show you around inside."

Cannert obediently followed. Once they were in the building and inside the office, Davisson's demeanor changed from accommodating to commanding.

"Sit there in that chair, old man. Tell me exactly where you're from and why and when you came here to Centralia. And you better not lie to me." He shook his head. "I watch around me careful and I think I've seen you before in and around my neighborhood."

Cannert gave him a surprised, frightened look. "I live in an upstairs apartment at 114 Allen. I came here from Chicago. I don't remember seeing you before, sir, but maybe walking . . ."

"I've seen you," Davisson said. "I live right off Allen myself. That's all of it, then? You're retired and sick and you moved down here? Why Allen Street? Tell me the truth or I'll make you sorry."

"I'm already sorry," Cannert said, feigning both bewilderment and fright.

"You don't have any relatives or friends here in Centralia?"

"No. None. I've met a few old folks in bars or at a dog track. I like to bet the dog races." He gave Davisson an uneasy, concerned look. "I'm pretty sick with cancer. If you want the money I carry, I'll give it to you."

"I'll appropriate it anyway for the cause," Davisson said coolly. "No hurry on that. Do you know anything about animal foods?"

"No, sir. Why would you ask me that?"

"They're made from grains, mostly corn. You add chicken, beef, pork, even horse meat. Our brand sells good because it has more meat and bone content than others. Dogs like it. Outside this office, in the plant, there are big machines that grind and mix. They also reduce animal bones to powder, form it into the mix, then cook and bake small dog biscuits. I'm going to feed you into those machines. In a few hours you'll be in sacks. Your bones and body will be ground up and cooked under pressure, mixed with thousands of pounds of other meat and grains. You'll be worth a hell of a lot more then than you are now."

"You're joking," Cannert said softly.

"No. I never joke these days." Davisson pointed to the office door. "I'll just drag you out to the first machine beyond that wall." He was enjoying Cannert's discomfort. "There's a hoist I can use to haul you up and into the raw mix once I get you dressed out and readied. The machines cook hot. I like to put old ones, male and female, inside the preliminary cooker while they're maybe still alive. I can watch what happens to them and they can see me through the thick plastic window in the front of the machine."

"I read something in the papers," Cannert said emptily. "I almost didn't come here because of it. You've done this to people before."

"Lots of times." Davisson smiled with open superiority. "Perfect killings. No evidence because no body is ever found. My company pays me bonuses for efficiency, and so you old fools do double duty for me. I get rid of you and make money on you at the same time."

Cannert sat quietly, feigning disbelief.

Davisson continued, warming to the sound of his own voice pronouncing judgment. "I read the other day that retirees have slowed down moving into my town of Centralia. I guess I caused some of that. You and the others should have gone somewhere else, fouled their water, used up their fresh air, and found a more friendly place to die. If I get you ancients stopped, then I'll maybe start on the damned foreigners. Before I put you in the machine, I'm going to do some unpleasant things because it's a part of your punishment for being here to bother me, plus it's my personal hobby. I like hurting and you'll hurt, but it'll be over soon. In doing what I do, I'll find out for certain all there is to know about you. Then, when you're up in the machine, I'll press these buttons here, one every time the light above it turns green. A computer can do it, but I don't like to let a machine do my personal cooking. In less than a dozen hours, you'll be part of our best and most expensive dog food."

He glanced over at the board, calculating. "Your bag numbers should start at about 6,151,200 and run on for several hundred bags. Tomorrow, they'll load you out to market, and pampered pet dogs will eat up the evidence."

"Those buttons there?" Cannert asked, as if not comprehending.

"Yes," Davisson answered deliberately. He opened his package. Inside there was a coverall, a long iron rod, and an evil-looking whip. "I went prowling tonight and you popped up as my personal guest. An old fart driver in a worn-out vehicle, a damned danger on the road."

"My wife Martha vanished down around here," Cannert said. "Handsome woman, gray hair, horn-rimmed half-glasses. She drove a Plymouth with Illinois plates."

Davisson shrugged. "Too damn many of you. Way too damned many. Most of you go where you can smell the ocean, but some of you come here. I hate you and I also hate all the damned foreigners. If I fail in my job, Centralia will have too much blacktop and too many trailer parks and condos. People like you will shuffle here and there, messing up the looks of my town, overfilling our hospitals and cemeteries. But not if I can stop it."

"Do you remember my wife? Did you bring her here?"

"I don't know. I don't particularly remember any of the ones I've brought here. If I cooked her, then you'll soon join her." He nodded grimly. "It's going to start happening now." He picked up the iron rod. Cannert saw it was barbed. "We'll start with a taste of this."

Cannert rose quickly to his feet.

"Stay in that chair," Davisson ordered, perhaps surprised at Cannert's quick move.

Cannert saw that the man wasn't completely sane. "Might I kneel and say a final prayer?"

Davisson considered the request and then shook his head. "There's no God inside here. You can pray only if you pray to me, old man. No other deity."

"I'll pray that you end my pain swiftly," Cannert answered carefully. He slid onto the floor by the chair and got to his knees and said his prayer for the dying. For a small moment, his body hid his hands.

It became time enough.

Davisson had been warrior enough that Cannert gave him a touch of his own blood to keep him quiet after death.

From a busy UPS branch office in Tampa, a week or so later, Cannert sent Davisson's driver's license to Lieutenant Ryan, c/o the Precinct Bar and Grill. He sent it inside the dog with monocle sack—mostly dog food, but also a bit of Davisson. A wary clerk closed the sack, following the new rules after 9/11.

He knew it wasn't intelligent to send the sack to Ryan, but it was something he wanted to do.

He moved on. He believed he was getting weaker, but he was still seeking.

- 4 -

Pursuit

Lieutenant Tom Ryan, a veteran officer of the Centralia Police Department, awoke to a ringing noise and inspected the semiruins around his rumpled bed without enthusiasm. Since his wife had divorced him two years back, after she'd found true love with a heavy-drinking car salesman, Ryan hadn't discovered the knack of keeping things in decent order. His apartment was a conglomerate of clothes on chairs, newspapers piled high on the floor, dirty drinking glasses, well-used shirts, dishes, heaped ashtrays, a few with crimson butts, and Burger King Whopper (his favorite sandwich) wrappers.

His rooms smelled of mold, mildew, and garbage. And of scotch. His apartment was, he believed, a ruined area, just as he himself was a ruined person.

His damned cell phone was still ringing. That was what had awakened him.

He answered the phone. He had a medium-sized hangover, not bad, but also not good. He fumbled for a cigarette but couldn't find one.

"That you, Tom?" Chief Todd asked.

"Yeah." The two men were longtime friends, both veterans of a local, feudal police system that gave few rewards for merit and exacted few punishments for stupidity. What it did best was teach survival. Todd and Ryan were survivors.

"You said several times you want to go chasing after that old dude you talked to in the Precinct Bar? The one you figured likely officiated at the final rites of our now dearly beloved Dog Food Davisson?"

Ryan said, "Yeah, I do."

Todd paused for a long moment. "Maybe we can work a deal. But first off I need to know if you're really interested. I hope you are, but you had no use for Davisson. He sued you and then sued the city of Centralia along with you a couple of times."

"He died before he won or collected a single dime, and his nuisance lawsuits died with him. Let's say I'm damned curious how anyone who looked as sick and worn-out as the old guy I remember from the Precinct Bar got the best of bad horse Davisson."

"You should be happy Dog Food's dead."

"Much of the civilized Centralia world is happy, and I include myself," Ryan answered. "But a killing, even the killing of an asshole like Davisson, is still at least a Centralia, Florida, misdemeanor. I'd like to catch up with the guy who managed it. I want to find out how and why. Then maybe have him pay a heavy fine and get a stern lecture in city court from our local 'Six Months Suspended and Costs' Honest Judge Billings."

Chief Todd laughed dutifully at the joke about the local inept, greedy, and almost openly crooked nonlawyer jurist. "Okay, I believe you. And I'd like you to find him. Maybe the citizens' group can use him again. We got worse baddies than Dog Food. Listen then with care to my proposition. For now it's only talk between the two of us. I'll swear up the line that I never said a word to you. But I've been told to talk and you will quickly guess who did the telling. You *are* acquainted with the good mayor's nephew, Alvin Andrews?"

"Sure. All of us po' cops who work the local streets know Anxious Al real well." Andrews had been on the police force for two or three unproductive years and had many times demonstrated he couldn't catch a cold during the hurricane season. Andrews had flunked out of Florida State after his freshman year and was now working on wife number three. Yet he was a handsome young man who looked good in and out of his police uniform. He could also be counted on to help with life-threatening things like the control of snarled traffic after the annual Centralia Fourth of July parade. He definitely couldn't be counted on for any dangerous police work. Andrews was a double dummy who hadn't made it at Florida State on a football scholarship while studying as a phys ed major.

He was also a joke and a danger as a police officer.

"He's bitten just now by the ambition to be a lieutenant. More than that, our upright and kindly mayor wants him to be a lieutenant. There's no opening just now for a lieutenant, as you and I both know. You have twenty-four years in and can retire next year if you want. If I dropped you back to detective sergeant, and you took the drop without protest, I could both promise and encourage you to go look for the guy who baked Dog Food into his final canine bites. The rank shouldn't mean much to you. You'd lose maybe thirty a month in pay up front. What they do on retirement is take all the ranks you've had from patrolman on up, figure what each pays on date of retirement, then divide them by years served in various ranks, so it'd mean maybe a buck or two a month less on your retirement."

"Are you dead certain that's how they do it?"

"Yeah. That's the tried-and-true formula. I got the DOR regs in front of me. And we did a retirement last year on Bubba Ben Sydney. I checked it against that also."

"Sounds all right to me just so long as my record doesn't show I was reduced in rank because I did something wrong like maybe conspiring with Dog Food to sue the city. How about we say on paper that I requested the transfer?"

"Good thought," the chief said stolidly. "There ain't a lot of money in the budget for travel, but I'll get the mayor to okay some being transferred from office equipment or somewhere after I tell him we got a deal. There's a city credit card you can take with you to buy gas, food, and stay in motels. Just don't live it up fancy and, for God's sake, don't put a drop of booze on the card. If the trail goes stone-cold, you got to privately promise me you'll give up your absentee life and come back here to finish your allotted time on the streets of sweet Centralia."

Ryan smiled and crossed his fingers in front of his eyes. "Okay. I'll take the deal. Whisper to the mayor he also ought to transfer extra funds to liability insurance if his nephew's going to be a lieutenant and more in charge."

"True, but I guess it ain't smart for me or you to inform the good mayor on that," Chief Todd said philosophically. "When do you want to go?"

"Soon. As quick as you can get all the okays. Anxious Al can go ahead and buy his lieutenant's bars, because I won't give him my old ones. What's going to happen first time he can't get out of attending a violent crime in progress or has to arrest someone?"

"Lord God knows. Probably nothing good. Most likely he'll get someone's ass shot off. Likely not his own ass, but someone's."

"True," Ryan said, mimicking the chief. He lowered the cell phone and found his cigarettes.

"Why'd you ever have that dog food analyzed?" the chief asked.

"I'm a cop and I was curious. UPS delivered the dog food package and Davisson's driver's license to me at the Precinct Bar, which was where I'd met the newspaper dude. And then I remembered the old guy asking me a bunch of questions about Dog Food."

"Just don't go after him real hard. Anyone who killed Dog Food can't be all bad," the chief finished. "And, the way things are in this poor town and county, we don't want to have to pay lawyers for defending a truly useful criminal, one who did our scut work for us and got rid of one of our menaces. Maybe you can talk him into coming back on a contract."

"I hear you."

"Remember also last fall I went to a national chiefs' convention," Todd said. "I told you about it when I got back, but I'll tell you again now. The word I got quiet-like is either kill someone like Dog Food's killer or give him a medal, but don't spend big county money trying him. And he might be the answer to the citizen group's prayers."

Both men laughed.

Five days later, Ryan used the Xerox machine in Centralia's friendly city clerk's office and made extra copies of a sketch he'd drawn. It was, as best he could recall, the likeness of the man who'd questioned him about Alfred Dog Food Davisson, all questions asked in the dimness of the Precinct Bar. The sketch wasn't very good because Ryan wasn't much of an artist, but it was better than nothing at all. The drawing didn't catch the questioner's eyes, which Ryan remembered as intense, zealous, and maybe sick.

He gave up his apartment and stored most of his stuff in a rented storage garage, one of hundreds built at the edge of Centralia.

Leaving town didn't bother him. The years of heavy drinking had cost him many of his friends. If he could stretch out the search, he might never have to come back except to collect the rest of his gear and officially file his pension papers. He liked to fish, loaf, and read, mostly science fiction, mysteries, and war books. He liked to watch sports on the tube, and he liked, more than all else, to drink scotch whiskey. The pension would give him enough to do all those things in moderation.

Next year he'd be finished as a cop. Maybe he'd get a private license and go into business. He'd talked with the chief on that. He knew he was good at being a detective when he wasn't drinking. And he could stop drinking. Sure.

He decided to drive his own car, liking his eight-year-old Chevy better than the already beat-up newer department surveillance Ford.

He got onto Interstate 10 and drove away carefully, not pushing it hard in the sometimes crazed traffic.

He took clothes, shaving gear, his fishing equipment, plus his extra pair of black Rockports with the spare orthotic inserts. He also took along half a dozen books and magazines from his shelves, stuff he'd only vaguely perused.

He checked in with the Tampa police. A bored, black captain at the main headquarters, dressed in a uniform as rumpled as Ryan's suit, talked carefully with him. There were no ashtrays around, so Ryan kept his cigarettes in his pocket.

"I'll have the sketch you gave me copied and shown to the people at the various substations and hospitals. Maybe someone will remember they've seen someone who looks like your drawing," the captain said, not seeming to believe his own words.

"He shipped the dog food bag from here by UPS," Ryan said. "It was an extra-size bag and it would be unusual to send a bag of dog food that size because you can buy stuff just like it in a store cheaper than you can ship it. You mind if I go around to your various UPS pickup locations by myself and see if I can learn anything? Maybe someone will remember seeing it or him."

"Be our guest. We don't care what you do around here as long as you get someone from this department to go along to make any local arrest. You got the UPS label?"

"I had it, but the whole damn bag of dog food got lost or maybe stolen from the evidence room after I turned it in."

Probably taken by a cop with a pet dog, Sherlock. The chief had a big Lab, and many others also had canines. The story about bits of Davisson in the dog food bag had been kept fairly quiet locally. The thief, even if he was a cop, might not know his dog was now part cannibal with an already acquired taste for humans.

The black captain laughed sympathetically. "Damn all evidence rooms."

"You bet," Ryan said, smiling only a little. It was safer to put evidence in your drawer, but you couldn't establish chain of custody in jury trials if you did that. And there were big criminal trials now and then, even if they cost the county big money. Some cop had seen the bag of dog food, maybe even heard the story on it, and then coolly taken it to save a few bucks on feeding Fido. Ryan wanted there to be no trial for someone who'd killed Dog Food. If the perp pled out he might do minor time, but the citizens' group that made policy for the police department would never stand for a costly jury trial. Ryan agreed with that and them.

"There's maybe four dozen places in Tampa where you can drop off UPS stuff for shipment. Plus many more in Saint Pete and the rest of the area, Largo, Clearwater, and the beach towns."

"Yes," Ryan said, nodding, "I guessed that. But I'm in no big hurry. I'll check them all out."

"You know this guy you're looking for personally?"

"Not really. I met him one time and he pumped me for information on the guy we think he likely offed. Claimed he was a retired newsman from the North, a long way away from Florida."

The captain gave Ryan a sudden doubtful look. "We don't want no newspaper troubles. You'll promise to call me if you discover anything of interest and contact us if an arrest has to be made?"

"Absolutely."

"We'd need to send an officer with you if you locate your man. Last year a detective from Miami didn't call and get one of our people. There was a shootout with a couple of bystanders shot, and it hit the old newspaper and television shows here. The lawsuits still ain't settled."

"Don't worry. I'll check in if there's anything at all. This perp's an older guy. My gut feeling is he's both calm and smart. He might be armed and dangerous, but likely ain't. I'd bet the closest he ever got to holding a newspaper job was reading the funnies. I talked to a few of the dead guy's acquaintances and coworkers. No one knew anything or remembered seeing my guy when I showed them the sketch, so this perp may be fairly cunning. I'm guessing he never knew Dog Food Davisson personally and came hunting him because of one of the area news stories about a bunch of missing old people. That means he might go after other baddies around here or elsewhere the same way. A bent twig."

"How old do you think he is?"

"Just old-old, late fifties up to maybe his seventies, but pissed off at the world and guys like Davisson. He likely came to Centralia because of the stories that got picked up in lots of papers. Davisson was a crusader against seniors coming to Florida and ruining our blessed state's small towns."

"Sure. Sure. We got folks here that despise all seniors, too." The uniformed man smiled. "We also got lots of folks hating other things like Cubanos, Mexes, runaway kids, and getting hated in return. Plus everone hates all cops. What'd you say this guy that got cooked was nicknamed?"

"Dog Food. He was a nasty piece of work. Big, strong, and meaner than a fresh-sunned snake. We're almost sure he did in a lot of old people the same way that he got himself killed—murdering them and cooking them after they were dead, then grinding them up and selling them as dog food. But by now evidence of all that is likely dog doo-doo. We checked out some of the dog food on the area store shelves, but there was nothing left." He smiled, thinking about Davisson's surprising death. Davisson had been a horse of a man and Ryan was much interested in how the thin, ill-appearing man he remembered from the Precinct Bar had gotten the upper hand.

He knew inside he didn't hate this older man who'd almost certainly killed Davisson. It wasn't even that this perp had used Ryan to learn about his prey. He'd thought about it some and decided the reason he wanted to catch the man was that catching crooks and fishing and reading were the only things he was much good at doing. He smiled inwardly and added drinking scotch. He needed to slow that down.

A contest. Ryan versus the aging hunter. He was certain that the hunter would never go to trial, would maybe cop a plea or get sent to a crazy house. Or maybe be of use to the citizens' group if he was mad at the right/wrong people.

He proceeded from police central to the main library. There he scanned the Tampa and Saint Pete newspapers, day by day, from before the time he'd been sent the dog food until now. He looked especially for stories about malefactors who'd committed crimes and somehow gotten away with the transgressions. He also looked for squibs about old people victimized, injured, or killed and stories where the old ones had turned the tables and won out over oppressors.

There were lots of victim stories. He scribbled down notes on things of interest. Strong-arm robbers were constantly stalking seniors who used the cash machines at banks, following behind customers and robbing them or doing the job right at the scene. Armed and merciless bandits were robbing trailers and casually killing elderly residents with knives or clubs whether the seniors tried resistance or not. Leave no witnesses behind. Repairmen and gas stations and drugstores also ripped off the ancients. The Tampa newspaper had a special column for subscribers to make complaints. It was full almost every day.

He found no stories in either paper where old victims won out.

He made a sheaf of notes.

Ryan found a second-class motel and checked in. He got his cell phone out of his bag after he'd put his clothes and toilet gear in the spartan motel room's bureau. His cell phone was issued and paid for by the department. The city council claimed such saved money.

He first called the UPS main office, the place where the big brown trucks were headquartered. He identified himself, then tried for information. People kept referring him onward until he found a friendly administrator who was willing to take time to talk to him.

"I don't remember anything personally about any dog food package being sent to Centralia from here in that time period. We might do five hundred packages a day here plus maybe a couple of thousand more that roll in from our branches. If it came into our central office, a receiving clerk could maybe remember, but I doubt it. We ship lots of odd things, but we seal it ourselves as per regulations since 9/11."

"Can you remember hearing about any animal food bags?"

"Sure. I can remember cat food, birdseed, and a hundred other screwy things. Most branch stuff goes out without our central receiving clerks ever seeing the packages. Our branch receiving clerks check it in."

"I got ordered to look into everything," Ryan said, trying to sound apologetic.

"Okay. You come to our main offices before four this afternoon and ask for me. My name's Worthem and they call me 'Red.' I'll tell the clerks what you're looking for and we'll try to help you. We keep a record on where things go and the records here also show who at which branch took it in. Whoever accepted the package might remember something. Was there, like, poison hid in the dog food?"

"No. The package came to me. And my finding out anything will make no problems for UPS."

"Okay. I don't want to help you to cause trouble. I retire in a couple of years."

"Hey, me also. Next year for me," Ryan said.

"No kidding?"

"I promise you, as one anxious retiree-in-waiting to another, that I won't make your rocking chair trouble and I also thank you in advance for any help," Ryan said. "I'll be there this afternoon. When I get there, can you give me a list of all your branch receiving stations?"

"Sure. I'll get it made up for you."

"With phone numbers?" Ryan persisted. "I want to move this beginning part of my investigation along."

This time the silence lasted for a time. "Yeah. I guess we got all those numbers here, or we can find them for you. Sure. Ask for Red."

Ryan dug around in his fishing gear. It was hours until four o'clock, and he considered finding a dock or a fishing pier and seeing what he could catch.

He decided against it. He got out a science fiction book club collection of short stories that he hadn't finished. He thumbed through it, making sure he'd not read many of the stories. It seemed as if there were some goodies left.

He put on his walking shoes after inserting the orthotics, took off the rumpled jacket, and slid on a thin windbreaker. He put the book under his arm.

Last, he checked his scotch bottle and decided there was enough for this night.

He'd picked his motel in a part of the Tampa–Saint Pete megalopolis close to water, but not on it or close to an interstate. It was an area full of old folks and cheap winter vacationers.

He left his car in the fenced-in motel parking lot and walked.

The area he walked was partly business, partly residential. It was full of 7-Elevens and small ethnic restaurants, inexpensive motels, liquor stores, and beach and T-shirt emporiums. There were also walls on walls of aging high-rise condos and apartment buildings. Old people sat lethargically in parks or on street benches watching each other and their decaying world without real curiosity.

Die warm.

It was what Florida stood for and what Florida sold to the rest of the world.

There was noise from cars and trucks and from an occasional siren, usually an ambulance.

Ryan sat on a park bench reading new and old science fiction stories. He also watched a mideighties man and woman sitting on a nearby bench. Both were stick thin. They had a 1.75-liter bottle of inexpensive Popov vodka and a half-gallon glass jug of orange juice. They poured a mixture into paper cups and toasted each other solemnly, no smiles, no words, no kisses, just silent toasts between old friends and/or lovers.

The park and its small world smelled of dead fish. Ryan ignored the odor and remained on his bench, watching around him.

The old couple drank and drank again, careful with the bottles, trying not to spill a single, precious drop. Once they saw him watching, and both of them silently toasted him.

Ryan smiled and nodded at them.

He believed they were octogenarian street people until he examined them more carefully with his cop's eyes. The Florida clothes they wore were clean and fashionable and the old man wore an expensive wristwatch. Ryan then decided they were condo dwellers hooked on late life orange juice and vodka, waiting together in the sun and ocean wind for whatever was coming next, alas.

After a time he left his bench and ate lunch in a small restaurant he discovered by following the aged lunch crowd, letting senior citizens lead him to the place. The food in the restaurant was plentiful. It also was at the edge of being inedible, overcooked into goo paste and therefore easy to chew and digest. It was cheap-cheap, which helped explain the crowd.

A McDonald's next to the cheap restaurant sat locked and closed. Ryan smiled about that.

He walked back to the park, but his old tipplers were gone, likely hiding from the burning afternoon sun in high-rise air-conditioning, napping, waiting for dark, death, or both. It made him sad to think on them so he did not.

The breeze had died, so Ryan removed his windbreaker, sat again on his bench, and read another science fiction story.

A few younger people wandered the streets, lost in the old folks crowd. They moved along quickly. Two young punks came ambling along, eyeing the crowd of seniors with mean, covetous looks. One of them spotted the seated Ryan and instinctively recognized him as a cop. The punks conferred and moved on quickly, turning off the main street at the next corner. Had they not, Ryan might have followed them. Instead he relaxed.

It was not his town and not his job.

Ryan looked at his watch and found it was well after two. He walked back to the motel. He sat in his room watching television game shows until it was time to go. He thought about a quick drink but decided against it. He seldom drank on duty. It was the only time he denied himself.

His new friend by telephone, Red Worthem, proved to be high up the managerial line at UPS. He had his own office and a secretary. He was tall and bent in the middle, and moved like a man with heart trouble, slow and easy, likely fighting stress and high blood pressure. He led Ryan to a less busy area and called over a younger, heftier man.

"You check?" he asked the man.

"I checked with some of the clerks. No one remembers anything like that being sent from here. But one of the loaders thought a dog food sack addressed on the bag itself might have come in sealed from a branch."

"This is the detective it was maybe sent to," Worthem said. "Can you tell him anything more about it?"

"No. The loader wasn't certain about what was in the bag but thinks it might have had a dog food label. Said he just kind of glimpsed it and thought it was odd we'd taken it without an outer wrapping, but them branches will take anything so as to get the money and look good on the books. He didn't remember the exact date or which branch it came from but did remember thinking it was a damn dog food bag and that the return address on it was Chicago."

"You want to talk to this loader?" Worthem asked Ryan.

"Later maybe," Ryan said. "For now, if you've got a list and telephone numbers for the branches, I'll take that."

Red Worthem gave him the documents with a flourish and accompanied him to the door.

"Good luck," he said.

"You also," Ryan said. He gave the man a smile and a salute. "Happy retirement."

Red Worthem smiled. "There ain't no such thing."

Outside the building, Ryan lit up a Winston. He reflected that he didn't want the forever-looming cancer, but he did still want his cigarettes.

He went back to the motel and had a couple of room drinks. He went out to eat but instead returned with snack food from a 7-Eleven. Inside his room he ate the snacks and thought about finishing the bottle.

Instead, he left the motel again and restlessly wandered the night streets for a while to tire himself. Once a small Ford truck with water skis tied to the cab top went past him, and someone young and burly leaned out the passenger window and yelled obscenities at him. Ryan thought about yelling back but instead acted afraid, scuttling up tight against a building, hoping that would invite the truck to return and he could deal with it and the occupants. He was still in reasonably good shape and hated punks.

The truck slowed but then accelerated and drove on.

Shit.

Ryan went back to the motel and slept restlessly after finishing the scotch.

In the morning, he walked to the beach, cutting the corners on a motel path that led to the water. He sat on the sand, thinking about the world and his own screwed-up life until the sun was fully up and the morning fog had dissipated.

When a liquor store opened, he bought himself a 1.75-liter bottle of Usher's scotch, a medium-priced brand he liked almost as much as Dewar's.

He sensed that the old man who'd quizzed him in the Precinct Bar in Centralia was not far away. He could almost smell him.

I will begin the hunt today.

He visited small hotels and motels in the beach area. He showed his pictures, and some claimed to have once seen a man who looked like his man. A couple of times they mentioned that the man had said he was from Chicago.

No one could give him a name, and no one knew where the man they claimed to have seen lived or might be found.

But it was a thing to do.

He hunted on. Later he took the Usher's back to his room and had a few while he tried to see out his filthy window.

"You're out there somewhere," he said softly to his absent quarry. "I'll find you. And then we'll see what happens. I won't let it be bad, old man. In fact, the way things are, I'll likely wind up trying to help you."

He went to sleep on that.

The very next day he met Barbara, and his life changed for much the better.

- 5 -

Gulfing

Cannert made up his mind that even though he was now growing tired of perpetual summer Florida, it remained the place where his lost, strayed, or dead wife had vanished.

He continued exploring the areas where he *felt* there was a chance Martha might have stopped or stayed.

He read and studied the newspapers from all the major cities and many of the small towns. He noted, reading about Centralia, that two child molesters had not appeared in court when ordered. He smiled about that.

Someone had almost surely killed Martha. He now believed that was fact, and it made the world grow darker inside him but did not make him stop his search.

If he could not find her, then he still might discover her murderer.

The usually warm weather and bright sun still felt good on his own aches and pains.

Florida mornings, except in the middle of scorching summers, were sometimes cool or cold. Those early hours made him recall younger days in faraway Chicago. He remembered the smell of Lake Michigan. It was much like an ocean in smell but perhaps not as sharp as the perpetual stink of the Gulf of Mexico.

He could smell the Gulf always, even when he was not near it. The odor was pungent, a mixture of salt water, dead fish, and too many people. He decided that it was worse than Chicago's smell.

He had lived poor in Chicago when growing up. His mother had been a good woman but a desperate one. His four-year-older brother had died when Cannert was nine, and his lone other sibling, a sister, had died soon after being born. His father had worked hard and drank hard, and his mother had been constantly sick. Both were gone by the time he was fifteen. He was full-sized by then, not big in stature but a strong, quick young man. He'd survived.

Now he was still trying to survive in Florida.

In the course of his wife search, he learned a lot about the Tampa and Saint Pete areas. At first he tried staying in the northern neighborhoods of Tampa but found that some of those areas, although much praised by newspapers as good places for seniors, were dangerous. Some of the businesses and their owners and workers preyed openly on the elderly.

Once, when he complained gently about a high prescription refill cost on his pain pills, he was escorted from the overcharging pharmacy by two white-coated drugstore employees who seemed more like hired thugs than store workers. He believed that only the crowds of watching and listening seniors close by saved him from at least a thumping.

The white-coated thugs first removed the cash cost of the prescription from his billfold, adding a bit for their trouble. They then ordered him not to return to the drugstore or even to the neighborhood around it. One of them then thumped his head with a strong, hard finger. His head ached for several days.

It was not enough to kill for in revenge, but he remembered it. He thought he could have taken the pair of thugs if he'd tried, but such wasn't smart.

He traveled away from that northern suburb and soon found a safer place in the south to stay and continue his quest for Martha.

On a night a few weeks after his retreat south in the twin cities, Cannert's old alarm clock brought him up and awake from the edges of a nightmare that was composed of the screams of others. There were Milwaukee men and two tough women in this nightmare, and he remembered them all well. Bombers and bomb planners.

They were gone now, dead, ashes to ashes.

The alarm emitted only a minor ring because its battery was low, but the sound made enough of a difference because

Cannert heard all. His hearing was still acute, and he could even hear the sound of his own blood coursing in his veins, thump by thump.

The hands on the clock said it was near midnight. Midnight had become Cannert's hunting hour.

Such hunting had early been in hot blood when his health and hopes were better. He would find his Martha still alive, and nothing would stop him from saving her from the bad people who held her.

He now realized the odds of discovering Martha alive had become remote. There were just too many people and too many places to look. Martha had vanished into Florida and the state's eternal sunshine. She was unlikely ever to be seen again, at least by him.

He couldn't seek help from the police because, by now, it was likely that someone official must have figured out that there was an illegal and dangerous searcher also hunting.

The police were probably looking for him.

He knew he was aging fast, and he believed that his body was also starting to fail him.

So, onward.

He hunted now mostly for those who might have caused Martha's disappearance or who now caused similar problems among his sheeplike brethren.

Some of the bad ones he'd discovered in this area and earlier places were now also gone to their own rewards. He'd sent them.

He was old, he was unwell, and he hurt a lot. He also was as tough as a rooster and careful as a fox caught between a forest fire and armed hunters. His hearing, sense of smell, and vision remained acute. So when he couldn't see trouble, he could smell it.

He switched off the alarm and turned on a naked overhead lightbulb. He did a short series of exercises. Some he did in bed, some were better accomplished lying flat on the cool hardwood floor. His body was still firm from long years of hard work. Some of his very early work had been as a laborer in construction, plus a few despised months in factories when there were no building jobs. He could still do almost anything in construction. He understood electricity, engines, and explosives. He could read a blueprint or fix a leak. He could drive a truck, operate a bulldozer, or run a crew of men. He could help a person in need of emergency assistance and he could bury a person who was dead. His life experiences and Vietnam had also taught him how to make people live and die.

The damnable exercises hurt, but he continued stubbornly on until they were complete. His breathing was elevated and deep. His movements were quicker and more precise than those of most men, even men much younger than he was.

When his routine was finished, he pulled on dark blue pants and a black T-shirt. He muttered curses against his arthritic pain. He forced the pain into a place where he could ignore it.

Standing in front of his bureau mirror, he examined what remained of Charlie Cannert.

He believed the cancer had slowed its process of killing him, but he'd also perhaps lost a few more pounds. Thinness had not yet moved to emaciation. but it was close. He remained strong, but these days he seemed to tire quickly. He thought on buying a bathroom scale to keep better track of his weight, but for what? Dying was likely now a matter of only weeks or months, if his several doctors and diagnosticians had called it right. And he believed the doctors.

Cannert's final answer was known to him, just not the end date.

He visited the bathroom. All accomplished there hurt, but there was no blood in his urine and there never had been. He took a pain pill and examined himself once more in the medicine cabinet's mirror. He thought he now looked younger than his true age. He believed that was mostly because there was little extra flesh left to become a double chin. And no wrinkles or jowls. He was now simply an aging, thin man.

He returned to his room and sat on the bed waiting for his pill to take effect. It seemed to take a little longer each time, and relief lasted a little shorter period. Or perhaps it was his imagination, as he kept no time charts.

He considered sliding back into sleep. He desired sleep. In sleep there were recurrent nightmares featuring bad people, male and female, those he'd exterminated while first protecting and then seeking his wife and the ones he'd killed in Vietnam. Their recalled faces intruded upon his dreams, but he suffered no true regret about their deaths whether he was awake or asleep. The Vietnamese hill people's holy man had taught him things to do about that.

He was without remorse. At times he even desired to add faces to the crowd.

He shook his head to clear it of the last of the sleep cobwebs.

He then armed himself by taking a long-barreled .38-caliber revolver from a hiding place under some clothes in the closet.

It drew near the end of the time he'd allowed himself to stay around south Tampa Bay. Time to move on, but moving on grew harder to plan. He was tired of both the hiding and searching, but he knew no better way.

He heard his landlady stirring down the stairs. She was ten years older than he was and somewhat disabled by crippling arthritis. She no longer tried to climb the steps to clean his room and bathroom, leaving him to care for his immediate area, which he willingly did. Her nonhelp was agreeable, because he was a solitary man and wanted no companionship from her and only a few words.

He did like her house. It was old for Florida. The walls were made of thick brick. Large trees shaded the yard and house. Vines covered with leaves and all-season bright flowers covered the bricks. The house air conditioner was quietly efficient. Once it had quit and he'd fixed it for his landlady. Now she came to him for all her fix-it problems.

Across the street lay a small park. Many times, when the weather was amiable, Cannert walked there. He liked to observe the children and young adults as they played games. It brought back memories of his own childhood on the streets of Chicago. On the occasional day when he felt too ill to cross the street to the park, he would gaze out the windows and see a little of the varying life. Basketball games mixed with young romances. Sometimes, when he felt exceptionally well, he would visit the park carrying and then strumming his tiny ukulele. The uke drew both kids and half-grown people.

Cannert loved all music, even his own. He also loved all the children. Plus dogs.

His landlady shook her head when she saw him exit her door with the uke.

"Those kids in the park see and hear you and they tell their parents and the word spreads to other people. All ages. One day someone will describe you to a curious police officer who's maybe read about you on a wanted list. The police will then come for you. That'll be the damned end of you, old fool," she said, worrying on it for him and for herself.

Cannert always shook his head. "What's your point?"

The old lady scowled at him and shook the three-pronged cane she used. "You'll get caught."

He nodded agreeably but doubted her prediction. Florida was full of odd, old, and ill people. Old people came to Florida to sit in the sun while they were dying and to hope against hope they really weren't going on dead and the fine weather would cure them. The police were both tolerant of and incurious about the multitudes of seniors. They had worse problems than the hordes of old people. Their world was full of killers, bandits, child molesters, and con men. Thousands of them.

Cannert knew that he and his landlady were joint owners of a single relationship named revenge. It was the only thing they shared other than her house and her car.

He'd read her name as a survivor in the Saint Pete and Tampa newspaper obituary notices. He'd first phoned and then later called on her at her fine shaded home. He'd liked the house on that initial visit and he'd also liked the park across the street after he'd moved in. At the corner of the street, part of the park and many of the nearby houses abutted the inter-coastal canal.

The landlady had lost her only child, a fortyish unmarried policeman, to the area's merciless streets. The police public relations people had openly blamed druggies in a news release for the policeman's death.

Three men had ambushed the son and his riding partner. They'd riddled the police car with steel-jacketed slugs when the pair of policemen had answered a faked emergency call. The partner had survived the deadly assault but would never walk again. The landlady's son had died in the car's front seat without ever firing a retaliatory shot.

The newspaper mentioned that the two officers had arrested many drug dealers. They then had paid the price for it.

Cannert had said the right words to her when they'd talked, and she'd invited him to cheaply rent one of her several spare rooms.

His landlady had seemingly not been much fond of her life even before her son was killed. Now she openly hated all the world around her with a consuming passion. She festered inside. Cannert had, for example, watched her smile when she watched reruns of the dark 9/11 day of the fallen twin towers in New York City and the Pentagon in Washington. Those buildings had lost their battles to ambushers attacking in huge, flammable airplanes.

Such reruns made him angry but left her smiling and exultant.

She'd also liked the bombs of the Iraq war and worshipped bloody people blowing themselves and others to bits.

Cannert remembered his own earlier Vietnam War and the hate he'd known and felt there. He'd hated his Cong enemies.

The two aging people had only the hunting and killing of their present days in common.

She owned a fine older-model Cadillac, dark green in color, old enough to be unobtrusive on the gaudy Florida streets where new, bright Cads, Lincolns, and expensive foreign cars abounded. Arthritis and the early stages of Alzheimer's had made it so that she could no longer easily recall how to drive and so he did that for her.

He also used her car at times to grocery shop and visit drugstores for both of them.

At night, now and then, he used it to drive to places they both wanted to visit, usual time just after midnight, shift change time at the police precincts.

Outside, in night's dimness, there was a warm east wind with a noseful of smelly Gulf in it. There'd been no measurable rain for two weeks. The Florida world smelled mostly of things from the Gulf.

Far to the left, Cannert could see the neon lights of a nearby neighborhood business section. He thought it was in Saint Petersburg. Farther away to the north and west he could make out skyscrapers and tall condo buildings, knowing them by their window lights.

Sometimes Saint Petersburg and its twin city of Tampa

experienced cold from incoming winds. Floridians called those winds "northers."

Tonight the weather was warm.

He'd early observed that no one slept nights on the metal benches or on the grounds of the park. The park was night empty. He guessed it wasn't safe after dark, although, at all hours, he saw police cars patrolling the area.

Such patrolling was a part of the police routine. No place was safe after dark. The Tampa north end was perhaps the worst, but all places were dangerous in the dark, even for a man who could see well.

His landlady said in her gravelly voice, "Good evening, Mr. Cannert." She never seemed to forget his name even when she spent long days and nights in confusion.

He said nothing but only nodded in reply. Her job was to provide the car and his was to drive it, then place it where she might personally witness bloody action.

She liked watching bad people get hurt. She liked even better seeing them die.

Since he'd moved into the best of her upstairs spare rooms, there'd been three shows, two of them good ones. The first show had been a failure in that the drug seller bandit had run away and Cannert hadn't shot at his fleeing back because there were too many innocents around. Next time, in a second foray, Cannert had gunned down a strong-arm bandit, killing the man with a single head shot that caused much blood to fall. Another time, not quite so great for the landlady, he'd badly wounded another thug.

Most nights there was little to enjoy except the cruising

from one area to another, watching, always watching the world around them. Cannert kept a careful look-see for someone who might be seeking him also.

The way many Tampa dwellers got their cash was with bank cards. The customer inserted the card into a large, metal machine, punched in the required personal identification number, and the machine disbursed cash.

Such could cause withdrawal problems for card users. Brute criminals, high on drugs, plied their nighttime bloody trade near the cash machines. Some high-crime areas of the twin cities now had television cameras that watched and recorded all, but there weren't enough cameras for all areas yet. Even where there were live cameras, police response was not always swift. The criminals, to confuse the issue, wore dark clothes, sometimes adding clown masks plus pull-down caps for disguise.

Cannert parked the landlady in a spot on a street. Empty cars were parked and locked in other parking spots.

He did an odometer check before he turned off the motor. They were about five miles from her home. That was far enough for him to feel secure.

Across from their parking spot there was a row of small, brightly painted business buildings constructed to blend into a beach area behind them. In front of those buildings were two ATMs. Cannert had been around this area several times before, but it wasn't one of the areas where they'd had blood action. He never returned to action places after blood had been spilled.

Cannert nodded at his companion and ordered, "Stay low in the seat."

She smiled at him, her eyes now as bright as a teenager's at a high school sock hop. She was as aware of the world now as she ever got.

He exited the car and turned into a nearby alley. She ducked down and he nodded approvingly. She could see but not easily be seen.

He could hear faint music in the night. Somewhere nearby a radio's volume inside an apartment or condo was turned high. Barbra Streisand sang in lovely trumpet tones, her voice as clear as a whistle. Cannert nodded, liking the music a lot. Streisand made him want to be Jewish, and he wondered if he'd been of that faith in some former life. He also wondered if he'd ever been of any faith at all. Had he always been an assassin?

He kept watch on the cash machines from his alley. He remained war leery of light and open spaces such as streets and yards. He remembered his old war and the lifesaving values of concealment in Vietnam, in or out of the tunnels, and how, in Chicago, he'd dressed in black and seen all, while staying unseen.

He crouched in a shadowy place near the street opening.

Hours of practice, dry firing and wet firing, had made him deadly with the long-barreled pistol.

A few cars drove in and used the cash machines without anything occurring.

The fourth visitor of the night drove a dirty four- or five-year-old Camry. The car sat at a curb two hundred feet distant from the machines for a time, motor idling. It then pulled to the closest of the idle cash machines, brakes squealing. There were two people in the front seat. Cannert believed the driver was a male and thought the person beside him was female. He also guessed that perhaps the pair might be going to try to crowbar a cash machine, hoping to steal its cache of currency. The machines were built securely, and opening them up was almost impossible, but strong-arm thieves still occasionally dreamed and tried. It took much time, and even the scattered, overbusy police weren't that slow.

If the thieves did try the crowbar ploy, Cannert would not interfere. He was only after robbers who preyed on human victims in their night games of life or death.

Sometimes Cannert would also tinker in the lives of drug dealers waiting to make a sale. Fire a shot. Turn a flashlight on them.

The scene Cannert watched remained normal.

The side window of the car rolled down. Loud music came from the car radio, but this music wasn't Barbra. A hand extended out and pushed a card into the cash machine.

Tonight no one hid out there in the dark bushes waiting to pounce on the cash.

The cash machine disbursed currency from its hidden supply.

A radio voice inside the Camry sang an old, loud song that cursed the world and all its bosses.

The door of the car opened and Cannert's sharp eyes immediately recognized the man who emerged. That man sang and lurched here and there as if he was drunk or drugged, inviting attention from out of the darkness, asking to be attacked.

The man Cannert saw had once been a police officer in a small Florida town named Centralia. Cannert had quizzed that police officer in a bar, buying him scotch and water, asking about a brute Centralia man who warred against old, sick people. That warrior killer had later died inside his dog food factory. Cannert had killed the man and then reduced him to bagged dog food, a fate the man had intended for Cannert and had meted out to other old people.

Ryan, Lieutenant Tom Ryan. The name came back to him.

Cannert took a small step deeper into the shadows. He watched intently.

He realized that Ryan might be cruising the darkness while looking for him.

He stayed motionless, afraid to run or move. He thought Ryan might have sensed him hiding in the dark and was about to search further, but the detective took a last look around and got back into his car. He was no longer play-acting at being drunk.

Cannert stayed in the darkness for long moments after Ryan's car was gone. He thought Ryan might drive back around for a final look. When that didn't happen and enough time had passed, he walked back to the Cadillac and tapped on the window for an unlock. The old lady complied.

"No more tonight," he said. "I need to do some thinking about future plans."

"Why?"

"The man in that car is or was a police officer from another Florida town where I once had some dangerous dealings with a bad man. He saw me in that town and he's quite likely now looking for me."

The arthritic old woman's face became pouty. She admired

their joined world only when Cannert shot people and she got to watch. She liked it best when he hit what he shot at and worshipped it when such person screamed, bled, and then died with her being a witness.

"Did you kill the bad man?" she asked, wanting to know.

Cannert knew she was no longer completely sane. He nodded at her and realized at the same time that such a diagnosis probably also applied to him.

Cannert thought more on Ryan. Had the policeman left his Centralia job and taken new employment in Tampa? Or perhaps he'd retired from the Centralia PD? Was he old enough? Could be. Maybe he was just on vacation? Had someone privately hired him? Why was he play-acting the victim? Had he been fired for his heavy drinking?

Lots of questions. No answers. Only wild guesses.

Cannert was certain about one thing. There'd also been a woman in Ryan's car. He remembered he'd been told that Ryan's wife had left him.

So . . .

For two days he stayed hidden inside the landlady's house. He went nowhere, not even to the park. He thought on what he needed to do. At times he felt ill, but it did not seem to be a symptom of a worsening of his cancer. He ate the white chalky wafers a doctor had told him about and took his pain pills and soon felt physically better. The nervousness receded.

It was time to move on.

There was a thing he had decided to do before his time in Tampa–Saint Pete was finished. Now was the time to do it.

On the third day he ventured out.

The north section of Tampa was as he remembered it. He bused there and took a seat on a park bench. The sun seemed unusually warm and the well-kept park around him was calm. The area was full of blooming flowers. Both old and young people were doing their things, but Cannert knew that what he saw was not always what it appeared to be.

Time passed and sunlight turned to twilight. Still Cannert remained seated quietly on his bench, watching the world.

There were now youthful thieves mingling in a multitude of seniors. The young ones were quick with both their hands and feet. Strong young ones would tear away packages the old people were carrying and scamper away. Cannert watched that occur twice and nothing bad happened to the thieves. Aged people yelled and screamed, but no police came. After a while the attacked old ones either left or seemed to forget why they were screaming. Cannert thought maybe the thieves recognized those with the worst cases of Alzheimer's.

There were no police in sight. That was good for the scamper thieves. It was also good for Cannert.

He wondered if the merchants paid the police not to vigilantly patrol.

He stayed near the pharmacy he'd once been escorted away from by musclemen in white jackets. At the time he was ordered away, senior citizens from the area had informed him that the scamper thieves, those who grabbed and ran, could return expensive prescription drugs to the pharmacy and be paid a good price for them. That way the druggist could sell prescriptions again and again.

On this night Cannert wore a white beard and carried a heavy cane. In his coat pocket he had a gadget he'd assembled. The thing was a match gun made out of two spring-type clothespins. Taken apart and put cunningly back together, the spring could be cocked to ignite and fire a lighted kitchen match at a combustible target.

Cannert had made himself expert shooting it.

Cannert didn't walk near or past the front of the building housing the big drugstore for fear he might be recognized. Instead he walked behind the store into a dark alley, surveying the piles of refuse.

Lots of things to set on fire.

No one watched or seemed to be lying in wait.

He decided that for the moment the wind was too strong and would blow out his aimed matches or turn them away from their targets.

He returned to the street. Seniors still sat on benches in the night. Some sipped drinks, usually vodka and orange juice, the preferred drink of the aged population. The orange juice was healthy, and he'd been several times told the vodka provided deep, sodden sleep.

A friendly pair offered him a cup. He smiled and accepted it. He drank deeply, toasting the couple. The vodka got his courage up and he entered the big drugstore. It was his number one target and he wandered its aisles, looking.

No one inside the store recognized him behind the beard, and he thought it was unlikely he or the incident was even remembered. He did recognize two of the brute workers.

He bought a bottle of lighter fluid, paying in cash. He returned to the street and walked from there back to the alley. The wind had softened to a gentle breeze.

He found success in the alley. He squirted lighter fluid from the can into and onto cardboard boxes and shot lighted matches at them. Soon, behind him, he left a trail of flaming trash boxes.

He heard an alarm go off. After a time, fire engines and firemen came. Police also arrived. When all were assembled, the flames in the alley were burning beyond easy control and the firefighters fought them with water and chemicals.

A crowd, many of them seniors, watched the scene with interest. Some of the young toughs who worked inside the drugstore exited and suspiciously looked over the crowd. No one seemed particularly to be looking for or at Cannert.

Cannert watched it all, hiding his enjoyment. He waited until the fires were controlled and the police and fire vehicles had driven away. By then the crowd had mostly vanished. He napped for a few moments on a bench, head down. Then he extracted the lighter fluid can and more lucifers from his pocket and used them once again down the alley, walking along quickly this time through. The only watchers now were a few groups of old people heavily into alcohol. They saw him with glazed eyes. They were snorers and drinkers, now awake and fascinated by renewed flames. One or two of them applauded him.

Cannert walked away from the scene.

He caught the late bus and watched backward until the fire scene was out of sight.

Returning fire trucks passed his bus. They came more quickly this time. The fire seemed to have spread to the inside of the drugstore building.

It was late. Cannert's final look indicated there seemed to be lots of flames inside the drugstore.

Cannert hoped the drugstore wouldn't ever reopen.

It was time for him to leave Tampa and Saint Petersburg. South. Maybe Naples.

6

Home Sweet Home

Until it was almost time for his bus to leave, Cannert stood across the street from the Tampa station. He found a shadowed spot in an alley and observed all until he was certain the bus station was not being watched.

He then purchased his ticket and boarded the bus south. The ticket was for all the way to Naples, but he intended to maybe get off the bus north of that city.

He used his on-bus time to reread newspaper clippings, particularly a series of stories he recalled about multiple mysterious deaths at a big nursing home north of Naples. The home's death rate was statistically far too high for normality, but no one seemed to be able to find any good or bad reason for it.

It could be that his vanished wife Martha was a patient there or had been there and been one of those who'd died under what were suspicious circumstances.

The news story was reason enough for curious Cannert to take a look.

Cannert believed there might now be more than a single searcher trailing him. It was time to move on and find a new place to hide and also seek. Also he was tiring out, his body shutting down.

He wondered if any searcher had by now discovered his identity. He decided to use his own name and social security number. It was chancy, but so were the alternatives.

He still had money. Much of it now was in the form of gold, the remainder in a wad of hundred-dollar bills. The value of the gold had risen and the purchasing power of the hundred-dollar bills had fallen. All in all, total value was around twenty thousand dollars. He carried it in his suitcase. His long-barreled revolver was now in a safe-deposit box at a bank in Saint Petersburg. He might need it again, but when checking into a nursing home as a patient, it was not good to try to smuggle in a gun. Besides, he could fashion a deadly weapon out of any table utensil.

After hours on the bus, at a road sign for Vanderbilt Beach, north of Naples on U.S. 41, he exited a mile or so east of an imposing group of high-rise condos that lined the Gulf beach and blocked out seeing sea and lower sky. There were also several huge trailer camps on a side road, that terminated at a small beach exit, plus coveys of double-wide homes and trailers scattered here and there between.

He began walking toward the trailer camps, carrying his suitcase. He returned to the highway only after his bus had vanished from sight. He figured if anyone remembered him leaving the bus, they might also remember both the condos and the trailer camp and his walking in that direction.

He thought it unlikely anyone would remember. There were so many people in Florida. The cities and towns were overfull of vacationers and new residents, old and young, all seeking the sun and, of course, health and happiness.

He walked a mile or so on toward Naples. Walking was not easy. He faked a gait that made him seem to be clumsy, slow, and handicapped.

Onward, Cannert. The fading hope of finding Martha made him keep going.

A day later he sat in an issue wheelchair as a patient, new address Suite 311, Good Gulf Waters Nursing Home. He was five thousand dollars poorer. The remainder of his bills and all the gold coins were in a fragile lockbox with him holding what he'd been assured was the only key. He hoped such was true but was uncertain. The property nurse had opened the room door to the double row of lockboxes with a simple skeleton-type key. That had disturbed him.

"We'll see what help we can get for you from Medicare, Mr. Cannert," the strong-looking lady director had informed him. "We'll show your five thousand dollars as a deposit only. Maybe you'll get it all back." Her eyes revealed clues to him that such was unlikely.

He watched her scribble something in a record book. He didn't think the figure she wrote was five thousand, but he said nothing. He was where he wanted to be for now.

"Do you feel all right in your new wheelchair?"

"Much better," he lied. "I was getting tuckered out. My legs were about to give up the fight."

She smiled without any meaning at all, a busy nursing home director smile.

Cannert smiled in response. He first intended to search the huge home for Martha. He felt safe again from most possible pursuers. He would also, at the same time he searched, look for someone who might be the cause of the high nursing home death rate. That person might have already killed his Martha. The problem was that old people and sick people were always dying.

Eventually, questions answered, work complete, he'd vanish again, his trail older and colder, his new intentions unknown.

In this downtime he had hopes of gaining new strength. Yes, he'd certainly do that. He'd sit anonymously in the sun under his old pulled-down Chicago Cubs baseball cap, drink cold, freshly squeezed orange juice, and rest his tired bones. He'd not worry about a thing. He'd eat wholesome, filling food and sleep a lot. The cancer would improve, maybe even get well.

Sure it would.

Six months to a year of life forecast, with now several months past.

Time of death would soon be past due.

Cannert discovered that things weren't going to go exactly as he'd planned. First off, he found that his Martha wasn't being held on the premises as some sort of captive. He checked every room, some of them more than once.

He did see one female patient as he rolled about, who startled him. She resembled his vanished Martha. But the nursing home inmate lady was at least a hundred pounds heavier and a good ten to fifteen years younger than his Martha.

If Martha had visited this place, he decided she'd have quickly fled it. The food was tasteless, overcooked, and sometimes offensive in sight and smell. He quickly tired of it. Only the frozen, not freshly squeezed orange juice was palatable.

If he wanted to rest or try napping outside the nursing home in his wheelchair, he must first roll to an exit door, get it unlocked by a reluctant nurse or attendant, then journey down a wheelchair ramp onto shifting sands. That meant trouble with overbearing attendants and nurses who argued his health would be better served by playing bingo or wearing himself out taking mild, indoor group exercises. He could also, if he desired, listen to various jackleg preachers' lamentations and pious prayers about a coming Armageddon or hear inept musicians' notes. Those were the everyday activities inside the nursing home.

When he forced things to go his way and escaped outside, he was attacked by swarms of stinging flies and/or sea gnats that wanted to own his body. Plus a white-hot sun that caused him to break out with prickly heat in his private areas.

His room was as bad as outside. He shared Suite 311 with an Alzheimer's patient named Ralph, last name unknown. After a couple of tries he realized Ralph would never notice or hear him. The bedfast man did only what he was prodded into by sometimes cruel nurses and attendants.

The nursing home smelled perpetually of human feces, mixed with rotten garbage, sickness odors, and the scents of the dead and dying. That was partly because most of the patients seemed to be there to die, living out their final days, waiting for the dreaded dark man with the scythe, doing it knowingly or unknowingly.

Several times nurses asked him if he wanted to talk to an area doctor. He declined, already knowing *his* own medical answer.

Three people died during his first nursing home week, one of them a woman only four rooms to the left of Suite 311. He listened to patients talk about the deaths, most information coming from a friendly, toothless lady named Ethel who lived right and up his hall seven rooms. She had bright, intelligent eyes and a wide mouth, and she loved to talk, talk, talk.

"Did you know the lady who died near me?" he asked.

Ethel showed gums in her friendly smile. She was both a smiler and a snoop. "I knew her. She had the emfersena or something. She couldn't get enough breath inside her. Her roommate said she maybe phyxiated in the night. And I heard the other two dead ones were strokers."

"Emphysema," Cannert corrected. "Asphyxiated."

"Whatever, mister. It could also be that a dirty someone inside here cut or kinked her oxygen tubes. That happens at times. The nurses aren't saying anything, but then they never do. Some patients whisper she might have done it herself. And the stroker dead ones might have taken or been given bad pills if their deaths weren't real natural."

"Strokers? Bad pills? Why, what, and by whom?"

"Some people in here like to tinker in their own dying. They get tired of being sick and worn out and nobody coming to visit them. There's no one in or out left to look for or love. Some have memory enough to remember the pain from one day to the next. The ones who live the longest in here are the ones who forget all of the bad stuff every night because of old timer's disease."

"Alzheimer's," he corrected. "Like my roommate?"

"I guess," she answered snippily, miffed by his several corrections.

"And the lady who died was one who remembered pain?"

"I think. She groaned a lot."

"Tell me all you know," he ordered.

Ethel shook her gray head, now openly irritated with him. "I don't know near enough words to satisfy a true nosy like you even though I'm a little nosy, too. There's a fat lady named Gert Jones who's set up her talk shop day and night in an easy chair down by the admissions office. Sometimes I talk to her. She's friendly and she'll like you, Charles. She likes men better than women. You go see her. Some say that if you want to die and are hurting and real bad off, she'll show you how to get yourself dead. It's also told by some she used to be a real registered nurse."

"Oh?"

Ethel shrugged. "Not now. She ain't no nurse now. She's the same as the rest of us in here, only fatter." Ethel smiled, liking best the part she'd gotten in at the last word about Gert Jones's fatness.

"Where exactly is it I find her?"

"You can't miss her. She's built like a Christmas church hog but has the face of a left-behind angel. When too many people started dying inside here, the police talked to her, but real quick she quit answering them. They lost interest and stopped coming around to see her. You go talk to her."

"Okay."

She looked Cannert over intently and found something new in his favor. "Is it that you want to die, Mr. Charles? Is that it?"

"Not yet, Miss Ethel," he said, not certain about it. "Maybe not quite yet."

A day later, making sure no one was watching or listening to questions, Cannert approached Gert Jones.

Gert's big body spread over most of an oversized easy chair situated at the junction of several halls and close to the main admission office. From Gert's vantage point she could examine every incoming patient as he or she was delivered and also watch the critically ill and dead depart in hearses or ambulances.

Cannert saw that Gert was fat but pretty. She was younger than he was. Cannert had been attracted to her when he'd first seen her and he now remained attracted. She was the younger lady who'd resembled his Martha when he'd first searched the home. Martha had never weighed nearly as much as Gert Jones, but she'd been heavy. That was okay. Cannert liked big women. He believed being fat kept them healthy.

"I weigh in at a little over three and a half," Gert told him, her doll face filled with pride, her voice cultured. He saw that her hands were small and that her brown eyes, hidden deep in thick folds of fat, were bright and interested. He decided that she was both pretty and cute.

"Isn't all the weight bad for you, Gert?" he asked. He patted her hands because he could instinctively tell she wanted him to do that. He liked it also. It was like finding Martha's hands again.

"Maybe it's too much weight for a lot, but it don't seem to be too much for me. I got these pills. A doctor who's now dead from a cerebral vascular accident prescribed them for me. The pills let me float along days and nights, all the time being happy." She nodded at him, and he knew she wanted her hands and other locations patted some more and so he patted away. It wasn't sex, but it was close. "I sit here and keep watch because something inside my head tells me I'm in charge of this sick, sick nursing home world and all the poor folks that's in it." She gave him a smile. "I don't remember your wife being here in the home, but my personal world now certainly includes you and the rest of the fools and losers in this stinky place."

"Do you live in your chair all the time?" he asked.

"Yes, except for using the bathroom. They feed me in this chair, but I can walk and get around a little. Enough to go to the bathroom."

"Sure costs a lot to stay here," Cannert commented.

"More for some than for others," Gert answered softly. She looked around, making certain no one listened. "They accept welfares, especially ones they know are about to die. They don't show the deaths real quick on their occupant books and then split the money with the damn crooked state and county officials. Sometimes they charge for welfares long after they've died. Plus other bad stuff."

"What sort of bad stuff?"

She smiled. "Lots. They steal big inside these walls. They like me because I don't tell tales to health departments and I never complain about the food. I just eat it all." She nodded and then made a cute face. "Every shit cake bite."

"I got told that you help people who want to finally exit this world."

"Who told you that?" Gert asked, her face gone angry. She looked around the room again to see if others were listening while her body moved in ripples like a boa constrictor. She turned and peered around, watching all. No one seemed to be watching and so she went on, her voice lower. "It's a damn lie, but stuff like that could bring cops sniffing around here again. They came before, but I acted sick and they gave up on me, maybe afraid they'd make me die and there'd be more trouble." She nodded her head. "Sometimes I tell doctor and nurse stories to those who like to hear and learn about suicides and dyings. I seen lots of bad things when I was in nursing and I remember all of what I seen."

He saw she didn't fully trust him, but he also knew she liked his attentions.

"I'm interested in hearing stories, mostly about suicides," he said in his deepest bass voice. "I used to be a reporter for a big paper up in Chicago. I could maybe write some stories anonymous-like and we could split the money I'd get. Would that interest you?"

She inspected him and his wheelchair without a shred of

interest. She said, "I work for cash and not for promises of halvers on something maybe happening or not happening in the future. You know that big Bob Evans egg and pancake place over on U.S. 41?"

Cannert thought he remembered seeing the place and so he nodded.

"The long-legged lady attendant who swabs floors and makes the beds down your hall will stop at Bob Evans and get bottles of real maple syrup, not the damned sugar-free kind, and then will charge you a buck extra a bottle. She'll want her money up front. Get the syrup and bring it direct to me. I got a hangup on Bob Evans. I like Reese Cups a lot, too, but I like Bad Bob's best because you don't need to chew it. As an extra attraction I'll let you watch me chug a full bottle. Then we'll play hand patties some more and I'll tell you good stories."

Cannert nodded one more time. "When?"

She laughed a little. "Whenever. Bring the bottle unopened. Or something else just as sweet. I like good candy, but no peppermints and no damn sugar-free or low-sugar stuff, my Mr. Sweetums-pie."

Cannert nodded acquiescence. He patted her here and there in promise. Soon both of them were breathing so hard it wasn't healthy.

It took Cannert several days to arrange it. In that time there were two new suspicious deaths in the nursing home. Both of them were people who were, the hall whisperers' tales related, old and alone. One, not hooked on an alarm system, pulled the needles out of his arm at night and so expired. The other suffered what Cannert's hall friend Ethel described as a "bolt," which he eventually figured likely was an embolism.

There'd been other deaths in the home. They seemed to be natural and above suspicion.

Cannert spent the waiting time rolling his wheelchair down the mazes of corridors, looking over everything and everybody, watching all in the nursing home world. No one paid any real attention to him.

There were no child molesters, of course, because there were no children.

Gert never called out to him when he rolled past her, but sometimes she gave him a conspiratorial wink or blew him a rosebud kiss. Once he stopped nearby and watched her eat. She ate everything in front of her, and it took her less than five minutes. She ate with quick, determined bites and appreciative noises.

It made him almost sick to witness it. He'd tasted the food and knew it was no good. He knew also he was losing weight because he ate so little. He was surviving on snacks from the unhealthy snack machines that dotted the halls.

He kept watch around himself. He closely observed the attendants, male and female. Some of them were practiced thieves who'd steal anything and everything, even reading glasses and false teeth. Cannert's teeth were still his own and therefore safe. He tried keeping his reading glasses on when he slept to save them. The attendant thieves were skillful enough to pick them off his face during his recurrent sleep times.

Many of his sleeps were populated by dreams about those

he'd sent into the dust and darkness of death in wars and else-where. But the holy man in Nam had taught him how to make those encounters gentle.

He grudgingly paid an attendant two dollars for another pair of readers, this time on a chain. The resident thieves waited until he slept again and tried to steal the new ones. This time he did better and awoke when someone touched him. He slashed at fingers with a tiny part-razor knife he'd worn for years folded in his crotch.

The word must have passed he owned a quick knife, because he was left mostly alone thereafter.

He watched nurses and attendants at work and thereby learned how to use the number locks on the doors that led to the open sand outside. The locks had nine numbers, no zero. You pressed the correct one or two numbers of the month plus a five-number code and the lock would click open for thirty seconds and then relock.

He looked on with interest as Gert Jones chugged the bottle of Bob's syrup from full to empty. She drank the bottle in about one minute. Her breathing accelerated from slow to fast and her face changed to bright red. A nurse went past as Gert fin-ished but ignored the scene except for warning, "Gert! Watch it on the damn sugar."

"Good glop," Gert said to Cannert, paying no attention at all to the nurse. She clutched her chin and then her chest. "Hurts some."

She kept watching him. "I'm addicted to Bob Evans and

good candy and desserts even though I'm diabetic. Lots of sugar can kill me. Right now I just get sleepy with the one bottle."

He nodded.

They patted each other for a time and then held hands while she catnapped. Later she came back full awake.

"Tell me if it's that you want to die?" she asked when her breathing got closer to normal. "Cops are around here more than I like. Maybe in plainclothes now. I got to be real careful these days."

"I don't want to die yet," he said to her. "Do you?"

Gert shook her head and shuddered. "Of course not. Life's okay. And I have my work to do right inside here. I'm a professional, you know."

Cannert nodded. "Tell me more about your work."

She nodded. "There once was a lady in here who wanted true bad to die. She stole assorted pills from some patient rooms. One day she swallowed all the pills at once. They took her to the emergency room, pumped her, and she survived, but with only half her stomach working and in a lot of pain. When she got strong again she tried hanging herself in her room, but the sheet ropes were rotten like the linens are in here and she fell. She bloodied her nose and broke her false teeth."

"Did she ever make it?"

"Sure. She got smart and brought me a bag of Reese's. I stole a gun for her from a sick policeman's drawer. He had the baddest kind of cancer where you hurt all the time. He didn't sleep much, but I managed the stealing 'cause I can be quiet as a bankrupt funeral home when I need to be." She smiled. "The shot made a hell of a noise and a hell of a bloody hole right above where her belly hurt. Died her quick and good."

"Others?" Cannert asked.

"Sure, sweetums. The best ways are the simple ones. There was a man who wanted to die because his chest and lungs hurt bad all the time. One night he got into our kitchen and turned the gas on at the big cookstove and sat breathing it. Damn fool was also a smoker. He lit up his damn ciggieboo and got burned bad in the explosion. He came to me when his burns got a little better. I sold him a clothespin and simple instructions. He cut off his own oxygen with the clothespin. A ten-pack of miniature Milky Ways."

Cannert thought a moment and then asked, "Do you ever die people for relatives outside the home?"

She leaned toward him, her eyes gone strange. "Sure. Why not. Two Bobs or their equivalent in candy are my usual fees for anything more complicated than these suicide stories I'm telling you. If I have to help someone do it, the fee goes to three Bobs, one a week for three weeks. For relatives outside it's sometimes more, but I ain't always real choosy. I don't have to have the sweets, just the money to buy them. I've no money. This damn home takes all my social security even though the federal law say that ain't just and right. Nothing left for poor Gert except a stolen dessert or two and what she can make on her own in jobs." A tear came and fell and she used a Kleenex to blot it and then patted him lovingly while he patted faithfully back.

"How about police?"

"I don't think they or the people who run this home really

care about who dies or how many die. They ask smart-ass questions but don't give a damn. There's a world full of people waiting outside to get in here to die. This place thrives and makes big money."

They both smiled at that, for they knew what she said was true.

Cannert returned to his room after the talk with Gert.

He sat on his bed and thought about both the nursing home and sweet Gert. In the other bed his roommate lay with his lost eyes open but likely seeing nothing. He wasn't full dead yet but moving on toward the river Styx without even knowing that it was deep, cold, and forever.

Gert was the killer he'd sought, but he wasn't angry with her. Instead he liked her.

Still . . .

If he did her in by violence, someone looking for new signs of him might read about it in the newspapers, come to the nursing home, and so close the gap between him and a lonely, solitary jail cell. He hated the idea of being locked away while he still felt useful and could search for his Martha even if he was slowing down.

Gert was a killer just like many others he'd known. Gert killed for gain. And she could have killed his Martha if Martha had been a patient here and wanted to die.

He hoped and believed Martha had *not* been here.

At midnight two nights later, he dressed in his own road clothes and picked the simple lock into the lockbox room. He keyed open his lockbox.

His remaining money, mostly in gold, seemed to be all there.

He tried and failed to open the other lockboxes with his key.

His month of rest and hiding had a week to run. Then the hard-eyed nurse director would ask for money or maybe just withdraw it from his lockbox without saying a word.

He wanted no more of this foul-smelling, bad-tasting place.

He thought they'd recently even gone to a cheaper brand of frozen orange juice. Inferior frozen orange juice was the damn final straw.

The search of the lockbox room did yield a double set of nursing home books as an extra. They were interesting reading, and so he took them with him.

He said good-bye to Ethel and shook Ralph's completely unresponsive hand.

"So long, roomie Ralph," he said, sorry for the man, the home, and the whole dying world.

He rode his wheelchair to Gert.

She sat in the quiet, watching all around, a fat spider spinning her web, plotting sweet deaths by the dozens.

He kissed her hands and they patted. She smiled and murmured words he couldn't understand when he told her it was good-bye.

They were romantics of a different sort and now would be lost to each other.

He exited into the night. Once outside he walked, moving

along okay, not really missing the wheelchair he'd left inside. He could still walk well.

It was unlikely anyone from the nursing home would even look for him.

At a flea market near the beach, he bought work clothes and soon found a job puttering about a golf course–country club inland from Naples, shining golf shoes, cleaning toilets, washing clubs, doing whatever was needed. There he ate good cheeseburgers and drank iced tea.

The pro let him squeeze fresh-picked oranges from trees around the course. His taste for food came back and he even began to regain the lost weight.

In his time off he hitched to Naples and walked the beaches of the warm Gulf sea looking for his Martha.

He thought about retribution and punishment, but then he decided against it. Gert's rules of engagement weren't the same as his, but they were in the same business. And he liked her. When it got right down to it, he approved of her.

He UPSed the double set of black account books to an IRS area office. Later he read headlines and scandalous stories about those books.

The world outside the nursing home moved along almost as sweetly as his new fresh-squeezed orange juice did.

He was still failing, but it was a slow process.

7

Chicago, That Cannertin' Town

Once Lieutenant, now better described as almost retired Sergeant Tom Ryan of the Centralia, Florida, Police Department, found out more about his semiquarry, Charles Cannert, when he traveled to Chicago. That trip was done partly to determine if the Chicago Cannert was the man he was seeking to question in closing the file concerning the unusual death of Alfred "Dog Food" Davisson.

Ryan made a cell phone call to Chief Todd to obtain permission to fly to Chicago.

"Why the hell do you need to do this? Damn it, Tom, we really don't much care who killed Dog Food. Most of us are plain glad the bastard's devoured and digested. Such group should certainly include you. And besides, isn't this maybe killer the kind they advise us constantly about in those citizen advisory seminars and meetings, the kind of death we're told to ignore for the greater common good of the funding of the city, county, and police department?"

"Yeah, but as I've previously whispered lightly, murder's still a crime in the state of Florida even if the victim was someone like Dog Food Davisson. So is destroying the evidence of a killing by cooking the dead body into animal food. What's happened now in the case is that someone identified this guy I'm looking for from the drawing of him I sketched and have been showing all around the state. This witness gave me a name. He was pretty damn sure the sketch is of a man named Charles Cannert from Chicago. I talked about this perp with the homicide people up there in Chicago, and one of their detectives got very interested. He said they have a file on this Cannert, but there are no wants or warrants. He then told me on the phone that I ought to come and talk to this citizen action leader up in Chicago who knows this Charles Cannert before I went farther."

"I looked a long time ago at your totally bad drawing," the chief said. "It was and is a piece of shit. How did you find someone who identified a possible perp from something as poor as that damned drawing?"

"Pure luck plus perspiration, Chief. I showed my sketch to hundreds, maybe thousands of people. This one guy was sunning himself on Saint Pete Beach and drinking a Bud Lite when I showed it to him. He almost dropped the beer. He then insisted the drawing was a match for a Vietnam vet he'd known in Chicago and who he'd heard had gone chasing down here to Florida to look for a lost or runaway wife. That interested me." He waited for a moment. "I'll fly economy, Chief. I want to go and I think I need to go to help us locate this guy whether he's ever tried in Davisson's death or not."

"You're not saying you want to do this because you want this guy tried, then?"

"Lord God, no. It'd be a catastrophe. We'd likely be forced to appoint him a lawyer who'd want to dig into all that happened at the dog food plant and take depositions from all the families that maybe lost someone to our dead dog food king."

The chief was silent for a long moment. Finally he asked, "Any other reason?"

"The guy on the beach said that our man had killed zillions of Vietnamese in the tunnels over there."

"That interests me, so go, Sergeant. But that's my answer this one time only. No more frigging airline tickets. I have to explain your bills to the city attorney and the damned city council and I'm catching hell about such bills from both. They don't think you should be off looking for this dude, what with our local criminal problems. I also talked to the area prosecutor and he now ain't much interested. I think he's afraid you'll catch up with the dog food man's killer."

Ryan sensed something in the chief's voice. "Not interested at all?"

"Maybe he is a little because of the dog food part. He thinks a case like that making it into the big-time newspapers up north, even if it never goes before a petit jury, might help our tourism, but he knows and we know the county can't stand big defense attorney fees."

"I agree with everything you say one hundred percent, but our citizen group might be interested in this guy if he's really a man hunter. Thanks for allowing me to go. I solemnly promise it'll be just this one trip," Ryan said. "How are things in town?"

"Don't ask because even cell phone calls cost money and I doubt you're homesick, asshole. I will tell you that I think I might retire same time you do," Chief Todd said, his voice both worried and gone sour. "My wife's maybe got lung cancer. Two packs of Camels a day for forty years. Damn all cigarettes. So maybe we can be private eyes together." He hung up his phone.

Ryan now had a lady friend he'd met during his search. He left his new lady, Barbara, who worked for Big Brown, UPS, behind in her apartment in Tampa. He'd met her early when he was calling on the various UPS substations. He'd been smitten. She was a well-assembled lady of about forty-five years, a neat package, and she was strictly a social drinker. She'd been married once and then divorced from a drunken, battering bastard. She still bore mistreatment scars from the marriage, plus she had one somewhat damaged child. The child was a medium-sized teenage boy who was now a sophomore in a Tampa area high school. He looked to Ryan a good kid who liked to fish and read mysteries, science fiction, and war books just like Ryan. The kid still suffered from bad dreams caused by the battering father. Ryan had plans for that father if he ever came close and caused a second's trouble.

Ryan liked the kid and the kid liked him. He had no children of his own. He liked the kid's mother even better. He even liked waking up mornings without a hangover after he got used to it. He was now trying to give up cigarettes and having some success.

Ryan had sworn to himself and stated to others that he'd never marry again. But now he was considering it. He hoped and was almost sure Lady Barbara was also considering it. She made him want to feel close to a woman again.

He left his eight-and-a-half-year-old personal Chevy parked in Barbara's apartment lot and had her use her aged Toyota clunker to drop him off at Tampa International before she drove on to her job at UPS.

He flew cheap seats into Midway Airport and found the Chicago police homicide detective he'd talked to on the phone, Inspector Steve Compton. That cop awaited him with a welcoming grin and carrying a sign that read SGT TOM RYAN on a cardboard placard.

Compton had an unmarked police vehicle parked in the middle of a yellow zone near the airport exit door. A uniformed cop watched over it. The cop saluted Compton and nodded pleasantly at Ryan, then vanished into the mob scene at the airport.

The weather was decent for Chicago, except that the outside air had a big-city stink to it. It was a different odor from the Tampa–Saint Pete air but still a bad smell. Ryan didn't like cities or even big towns much.

Compton said, "This guy I want you to talk to is at work in his office now, but he'll make time for us when we get there. His name is Jimmie Webb and he was an army major who served with Charles Cannert in Vietnam. He now helps run a real estate company. The company rented Cannert and wife their apartment. And he's high up in the Chicago area citizens' action thing. It fights for and gets us money. He's a big-timer in this city and he's a friend of the police kind of guy."

"We've got a group like that. How high up is your guy?" Ryan asked, not certain where they were heading or why he was getting so much assistance in this huge metropolis, but still interested.

"Listen to him," the inspector said. "I think you'll soon see reasons for talking to him."

"You said you had no wants or warrants for Cannert. Is that still a hundred percent true?"

"I'll tell you again for sure and for certain that we don't want him. More than that, we'd probably try to help him if someone away from here went hard after him."

The guy who knew Charles Cannert had offices in a large suburban office building. Compton parked the unmarked car in a guarded visitor area and they proceeded silently together up to the eighth floor. A pretty secretary walked them down an air-conditioned, deep-carpeted hall and tapped on a massive office door that had a sign reading JAMES WEBB VICE PRESIDENT.

Webb was medium size and getting along into what Ryan thought was likely his late sixties. He came quickly to his feet and his handshake was firm.

"Here are some pictures I found. They're of Charlie Cannert and his wife. They were taken at an army outfit reunion party at my house last year," he said. "I thought pictures of both Cannert and his wife might be of use to you. You can take them with you."

Ryan recognized Cannert in the photos and became completely certain he was the man he'd talked with once in the Precinct Bar in Centralia, Florida. He'd never seen a picture of Cannert's wife and was glad to obtain it. He nodded at Webb.

"Thanks," he said. "You big-town people are sure a great help to a thirty-person police department in down-in-the-dirt poor rural Florida panhandle."

"Maybe both you and Charlie Cannert deserve some help. Do you know anything about Cannert's army record?"

"No, other than what I just heard you say about an army outfit reunion at your home, and the guy who identified him in Florida said good things about him."

"Charlie Cannert went overseas to Vietnam as a corporal in my guard outfit. He'd been in the National Guard for a while without impressing anyone much. He worked early on as a grunt. Outside the guard he worked a lot of other jobs, including a several-year jolt as a mortuary assistant and a year or more as an emergency ambulance driver and attendant. He used his own money to take training. As you can see in the picture, he's not a giant, just a medium-size ordinary guy, but he did giant things in Nam. He volunteered and became a tunnel rat in Nam. When the North Vietnamese would hide from us and the hill tribes after a fire fight, they'd manage it at times by going deep down into networks of interlocking tunnels they'd built. The tunnels were hard for us to deal with. The tribes were better at it than we were. When it got full dark the Cong would sneak out of a hundred hidden hole openings and night

— 125 —

ambush our people. Charlie had great eyes and spectacular re-
flexes. My sergeants used to swear he could see in the dark. He
was lightning quick back then with gun and knife, particularly
knife. He was, of course, a lot younger then. He'd go straight
in under the ground with tribesmen after the Cong and sometimes, several times even, the black clad bastards would have to
abandon a whole area of their tunnel networks just to escape
from him and his knife."

"Cannert was that good?"

Webb nodded. "He was awarded a Silver Star, plus two
Bronze Stars. He got a couple of Purple Hearts for wounds
suffered in the tunnels. He also almost got killed. We soon
upped him to sergeant, then master sergeant, and we even tried
once to give him a battlefield commission because of all he
did. He turned down the commission. He was a hero to the
big area tribe who were allied to the south Vietnamese and so
also to us. Those people, and particularly their religious lead-
ers, believed he'd been touched by their hill gods. The holy
man from the locals followed him all over outside the tunnels
along with an interpreter. They worshipped him. He learned
some of their language and customs. He lived with them more
than he did with us."

"Hot stuff," Ryan said. But he nodded, impressed.

"I wrote him up for all the big medals, including the DSC
and even the Congressional Medal of Honor. That was after
he brought back several of our officers who'd been taken prisoner. The awards got downgraded because it was that kind of
damned war, a war we didn't win."

"So he came back home as a hero, and you also returned,

and later he wound up living with his wife in apartments you run or own? And he went to your home for reunions?"

"He came back home as a critically wounded hero. For a time it looked like he'd die. A large corporation owns the apartments where Charlie lived. I own a small amount of stock in that corporation and I work doing business things for it. I'm one of several vice presidents. I'm a CPA, and I keep books. They pay me well, but I earn every dime of it. I've been offered more money by rival companies, but I like what I'm doing." He nodded. "Most of the surviving guys from my outfit come to the reunions. We hold the revivals various places. We had it one time at my place. We lost a lot of good people, and those who are left remain close. And that's what happened."

"I get the feeling that you and the inspector here think maybe Charlie Cannert deserves some kind of special treatment for going into dark and dangerous places and killing a lot of badasses?"

"That's not our reason for talking to you, but I guess it's the first part of it," Webb said. "What we mostly want you to know as a police officer concerns what he perhaps later did here in Chicago after he recovered from wounds. And then we hope you can figure out for yourself, if you're smart, why there aren't any Chicago wants or warrants for him."

"What he perhaps did?"

"Right. We don't know for certain he did anything at all, and no one in authority here has ever pressured hard to find out. It's unlikely anyone in the Chicago police ever will. If he did do it, he technically broke the law." He smiled a hard smile.

Ryan nodded and decided to relate a few things from Florida to maybe shorten the interview. The pictures were great and he was glad to have them. But he didn't need to hear good things about Charlie Cannert. He already favored him. So did his Centralia chief. He also was certain Charlie Cannert wasn't ever going to get tried by any Centralia jury.

He said, "Let me first tell the two of you something about what Cannert did, or in your choice of words, perhaps did, down in Florida. I hold inside my jacket pocket a John Doe warrant charging anonymous John with murder, but I likely will never serve it and have no desire at all to change that. I'm looking for John Doe or, we'll say right out in the open, Charlie Cannert, mainly to ask him a few questions and clear up a case. The questions concern a badass bastard who once lived and worked in my Florida town. His name was Alfred Davisson and his hobby was hating old folks, foreigners, and other newcomers who came to my small city. Davisson mostly and firstly hated the multitudes of aging tourist-type people who came and still come to visit and maybe to die in our Centralia sun. There are no beaches or ocean in Centralia, and things don't cost a ton. So old people come there and like it. We think this bad man likely killed some of our old-time visitors, male and female. We were investigating him concerning that when he got pissed about it and sued both the city and me because our investigation bugged him. Later he somehow vanished. We know he worked in his animal food plant all day on the last day he was seen in Centralia. He then disappeared. A week or two later I got a sack of dog food delivered to me in Centralia. We had it examined because the sack contained Mr. Davisson's driver's license. We found a fraction of a pound of Mr. Davisson cooked up and mixed together in the dog food, all very edible and sanitary. Whoever did Davisson in also dressed him out and destroyed the unsanitary parts of him before cooking the remainder."

Ryan paused for a moment, then continued. "Now this Mr. Davisson was a horse of a man. Your Charlie Cannert, who's not a horse of a man from what I saw of him then or in your old army outfit pictures today, had asked me some questions in a Centralia bar concerning Mr. Davisson. So Charles Cannert became a suspect in Davisson's death. If I find him, I intend to first off give him all his Miranda warnings at least half a dozen times and then ask him some questions. I doubt he'll answer my questions. Most people who've been Mirandized quickly decide they first want to talk to a lawyer. I intend to warn your Charlie Cannert that I think he likely needs to talk to such lawyer. I also intend to damn make certain he does talk to one. So, knowing that, do the two of you want to go any farther with telling me good and interesting tales about Charlie Cannert now?"

Webb and the inspector looked at each other for maybe a second. Then both nodded.

Ryan found himself much surprised. "Go ahead, then," he said.

"Charlie and his wife rented an apartment in this building we reserve for older people without kids," Webb continued. "The rent was and remains reasonable for the Chicago area. It's an old building, but it's clean and well kept and the people who live there like it and help take care of it. It's been written up in the Chicago papers several times because of what it is and what it costs. Maybe a year-plus ago now I had some callers come here to this office. They were three tough-looking men and they'd made an appointment before the visit. They said they had come to inform me and my company about some special insurance they were selling for aging buildings. I got told I needed this insurance not only perhaps for my own health and the other officials of this corporation, but also for the health of the older people in the large apartment building where Charlie and his wife lived. Let's say these salesmen quickly got my attention. They were firm in telling me, polite, but they talked mean and tough. I believed them and was afraid. To obtain the insurance I was told the corporation would likely need to raise, maybe even double, the apartment rents. I listened carefully, trying to learn as much as I could about my callers. When they were done, I told them to take a quick hike. I admit being very polite doing it. I remember believing they might kill me right then and there. Instead they nodded and smiled like they'd expected my answer. They said they'd be back in touch and then peacefully left the premises."

"Jimmie called me as soon as they were out his office door," Compton said, picking up the story. "I checked the names these guys had given and also their addresses plus the phone numbers on their business cards. The callers were walking, talking complete fakes. No such addresses existed, and no such phone numbers had ever been issued by any phone company. I had Jimmie go through the police mug books and we drew only a couple of maybes. We decided it was likely the men had come visiting from away from Chicago, maybe the West

Coast, maybe New York or Miami, but somewhere away. I had the precinct in the area run patrol cars past the apartments frequently for a time. Nothing happened. But when we went back to normal patrols, something did happen."

Webb nodded. "Two weeks after we cut back patrols, someone touched off two simultaneous bombs, one in the front, and the other in the back of our fine old apartment building. Big bombs. Blew out lots of windows both in the apartments and in other nearby buildings. Did damage. The bomb squad people said if the bombs had been set off closer there likely would have been multiple fatalities and they were somewhat surprised there were only two killed from the explosions that did occur. Cannert's wife and a couple of other people were slightly injured and, of course, two tenants died. A few days after the bombing we got another call about buying this insurance, a telephone call made from a phone booth. They said it was a final notice and they'd call once more and give us directions about how to pay the money. That's when Charlie got into it."

"Why Charlie?" Ryan asked, interested now.

"Charlie was the president of the Green River Apartments Residents' Association. He therefore was told about these fake insurance salesmen. He also learned most of the rest of what we knew," Webb continued. "Alcohol, Tobacco and Firearms people from the federals also got into it because of the bombs. They told us the bombs had been assembled by experts. They said similar threats had happened in eight other cities around the country, but as of that time they knew nothing more. No one had paid money, no one had been caught, and no one, other than us, had been bombed. After the bombing, we kept patrols coming and going into the area and assigned a large team of detectives to the investigation. We guarded the building. No one turned anything up. We checked out the guys that Steve thought were mug possibles but got zilch from doing it. I looked at other cities' mug books. Nothing. It stayed quiet. That's when we think Charlie Cannert might have found or seen someone, but he never told us a single frigging thing."

Compton cut in. "I do know that Charlie thought someone might go after Jimmie here. He and Jimmie were close friends because of Nam, and we believe he might have shadowed Jimmie from a distance on his own. Jimmie saw nothing. We don't know what Charlie saw, or even if he saw anything, because, like I said, he told us nothing. Maybe he did see something or someone and then followed up on his own. But everything just stopped."

"The problems ended. All over and done. No more calls, no more bombs, no nothing," Webb added. "No attacks on anyone, anyplace. No explosions, no bullets. We never heard another damned word. ATF eventually confirmed the same thing happened in all other threatened places. The problem just went away."

"Except . . . ," Compton added.

"Except what?" Ryan asked.

"We did find a couple of dead bodies. A decomposed male body washed up on the shore of Lake Michigan months later. The body had been in the lake for a while. Another body got found in a Milwaukee alley. It was in bad shape because the face had been cut to pieces, the facial bones broken and the eyes removed, plus all fingertips removed from both hands," Compton said. "Those bodies still remain unidentified."

"Was there enough left to guess if the bodies were of any of the people who'd tried to sell insurance?" Ryan asked.

"Not with any certainty. Jimmie looked the bodies over and just couldn't say one way or another. We sent the pictures of the bodies to the other cities. The only thing we got was both of the dead men seemed about the right size," Compton said. "Both had died violently, knifed to death. The one taken from the water was decomposed pretty badly. His eyes were also gone, removed. The one in the alley had been elsewhere, likely in other ground for a few months before being dug up and dumped."

"Did Charlie Cannert show any interest in inspecting these bodies?"

"No. We asked, but he declined to take a look. I remember he told us he'd found out nothing, seen nothing, and therefore seeing dead body pictures wouldn't mean a damned thing to him and would waste his time. We didn't push him, because this was right about the time he first started going to the doctors and found out about his cancer. The cancer later got worse and he went into a local hospital. They opened him up, sewed him shut, and gave him the bad news. Charlie's wife took off for Florida to find them a place and vanished down there. And afterward he got well enough to go looking for her."

"Is there a lot of time left for him?"

Both of the Chicago men shook their heads. "Unlikely," Compton said.

"I see," Ryan said. "Does anyone up here in your hierarchy

want to talk to Charles Cannert further, or do you want me to ask him any questions about any matter at all if I or we should locate him?"

Both the Chicago men shook their heads again. Then Jimmie added, "We have questions, but we don't need answers to them because our problem has gone away. What we're asking of you is to notify us if we can be of help should things go wrong for Charlie down there in Florida."

"I don't think there'll be a problem," Ryan said. "I've got an area prosecutor who might get more interested if he thought it would help him politically, but there are lots of things I or my chief can do that will turn him off and away." He looked at both men. "Charlie Cannert seems to be a most unusual guy."

The Chicago men smiled.

"Do you have other cases like Mr. Cannert's?" Ryan asked Inspector Compton.

"None just now," he said. "But the times make us more careful in things we do now. We've learned not to run around making everyone crazy just to stay busy."

Ryan looked them both over. "Of course. Our problems are much the same in Florida. We got a state full of killers, land sharks, crooks of all kinds, child molesters, and sex nuts. Thousands and thousands of them. I now plan to return to my lovely little Centralia. If I should find out anything of interest to you or need help, I may call one or even both of you on my cell phone, but only if there's true need." He nodded. "In these days when so damn many things can be problems, one needs to know what things really need final solutions."

"Exactly," Inspector Compton said. Both of the Chicago

men smiled, and Ryan felt the three of them understood each other pretty well.

Jimmie said, "One more thing. Some of our people went back to Vietnam on a visit a couple of months ago. They were allowed to take a bus trip to the area where the outfit once had been. The Vietnamese were in charge of the bus. They made our people stay on the bus because things were still dangerous. Looking out the bus window, our people saw several peculiar statues on hills and in towns. The statues were of Charlie Cannert. They were sure of that."

Ryan flew back into Tampa the same day. First he talked to Chief Todd. Both of the men now shared an interest in Charlie Cannert.

In Centralia he had numerous copies of one of the Chicago photos made. Ryan then sent the results on to police departments, state agencies, and any other place that seemed a possible source for information. The photos were not called wanted posters, only "wanted to contact."

One place he sent these photos of Martha Cannert was to all of the various Florida state mental hospitals.

He sent out only pictures of Martha Cannert. He sent nothing more out concerning Charles Cannert. He also decided he no longer needed to show his sketch and he destroyed it.

One of the state hospitals Martha Cannert's picture was sent to was Tepsicon Rest Hospital. That mailing brought dividends.

8

Jane at Large

Jane Doe became absent without leave from Tepsicon Rest Hospital by the simple act of opening and then closing behind her a basement door at a nearby town's library building. After closing the door, she walked quickly away without a single look back.

She was weary of living in Tepsicon and she realized that if she remained there her chance of ever finding a meaningful life was remote.

She exited the basement door and fled on a day when Odd John Dorwin was in charge of the library visitation patient group rather than when her friend Alma Dagley Jones ran the venture. She wanted no one to blame Alma.

She'd lost much weight in Tepsicon on its diet of oranges, fatty bacon, and homegrown vegetables and more because she had adopted the habit of walking and exercising a lot. She was now almost forty pounds under her onetime weight of just under two hundred pounds. She felt strong and well. And, for the first time in many years, almost unrecognized by herself, she had a figure.

Odd John, the security captain, had kept his eyes on her all the way to the library, but that was not unusual. He always watched her and she usually kept a wary eye on him. He was attracted to her partly because (and such was well-known among the patients) he liked tall women, even more now because she was a handsome lady.

She despised him mostly because he was mean and ugly. He also perpetually smelled bad. His breath was worse than his sweaty body odor.

Jane had vague memories of someone who smelled clean and good, and she thought that person had been a man she'd once known and who now was lost. She hoped to find him again.

When the group of patients were set free to roam inside the town library, she unexpectedly spoke to Odd John, approaching him boldly, wanting to make certain he didn't bother her or watch her too closely in the library on this day, which was to be her independence day.

"Come see me at the hospital tonight," she said, smiling at him for the first time. She touched his face lightly with her right forefinger and endured a double whiff of foul breath and body odor while she tried not to change her facial expression.

"But you damn well better leave me alone today while I read and study on some important things," she ordered, still smiling. "Just come see me tonight."

"Yeah, yeah," he said enthusiastically. "I hoped it would happen this way sometime. I like you a lot. I might even give you some money if you're really nice to me."

She felt like giving him a farewell fist to the testicles, but instead she smiled once more.

"Tonight," she said, trying to make her voice sound sultry like some of the female voices in the movies shown Friday nights at the asylum. It was hard to do even at her new weight, but she got the job done.

Buses ran from the town with the escapable library to Florida's west and east coasts every several hours. She took an early one to the west, knowing the schedule favored her going that way. The more quickly she got miles away from the areas close to the asylum, the better her chances were to remain free. The Gulf of Mexico was closer than the Atlantic to the town near where Tepsicon was located.

She remembered from past runaways she'd been told about that there'd been emergency calls from the asylum to area police and to state troopers on both coasts. Some patients were later brought back to Tepsicon by law officers. Others had returned to the hospital on their own or been brought back by family members. A few had vanished and stayed gone. No one seemed to miss them once they were away and gone.

Jane Doe hoped she'd be one of the lucky escapees.

It was now early spring. In this part of north Florida, daytime temperatures were mostly high fiftyish or low sixtyish with sunshine and clouds mixed. The nights were usually cool enough so that she knew she'd likely need shelter during the dark hours.

Soon it would be summer and all Florida would begin to swelter in the sun.

When she was off the bus, she headed west and south, walking in the quick gait she'd learned or relearned once she'd healed in body and returned to good health. She found a wide street and recognized it as a highway that ran north and south near the Gulf. It was marked U.S. 41 and she remembered studying it in a library map she'd tried to memorize. There were multiple stoplights and many cars on the highway. Beyond endless rows of condos and motels she could see and smell the waters of the Gulf. She would have liked to stop and watch the people and observe the water and the boats. Instead she moved on, fighting time. Get far away and get off the highway.

After several hours of hard walking, she saw a Help Wanted sign in the window of a motel. It was not yet dark, but it was nearing sunset. Anyone walking the streets after dark would likely be suspect. And they would now know for certain she'd run from the library and therefore fled Tepsicon Hospital.

She'd walked miles from the bus station. She was tired and hoped she was far enough away from Tepsicon so as not to be easily found. Besides that, her feet hurt.

She entered, taking the sign with her. She clutched it next to her suitcase.

A thin, elderly lady with white hair and wary eyes examined her from behind a counter and also likely saw no parked car near the office. She said firmly, "I'm Angela Cart, the manager here. We have no public toilets if that's what you're looking for. Would you be looking for a place to stay, ma'am?"

Martha shook her head and put the Help Wanted sign on the counter. "I'm looking for a job, whatever kind of job you have available."

The white-haired lady's face brightened a little. "I could sure use some temporary help. Do you know how to clean rooms? Will you do toilets and baths and get them good and clean? Will you not steal things from guest rooms?"

"Yes, ma'am. All of those. And I hope you'll notice I'm strong."

"I can use you and put you to work right now. You speak English rather than Mex. That's good. You do look strong. Fill me out this application form." She smiled. "And try not to lie a lot."

"I also could use a place to stay for the night. I have some money and can pay."

"You can stay right here in the motel tonight. This time of year, if we're lucky, we hope to run maybe forty percent occupancy, so there'll be no charge to you for tonight. Tomorrow we'll find you a decent little place to stay nearby." She gave Jane a worried look. "I hope that the police aren't looking for you for something bad you've done?"

"No real or true law's after me." She looked out the big window. "But a man and or some of his rough buddy motorcycle gang friends may come looking for me. Or he might try to send police. I had some trouble with bad men a while back in one of their camps. And earlier today I walked away from Tepsicon

Hospital. I lost some of my memory when I was badly beaten up by bad people several months ago, but I never hurt anyone at Tepsicon or anywhere else. And I hope you'll look at me now and listen to me and believe I'm not crazy."

"You don't look crazy," the woman said soothingly. "Did you run off from a husband or boyfriend who's a biker who swore you into Tepsicon?"

"Yes. It was exactly like that. Him and his heavy-drinking, drug-taking friends." She smiled, trying to make her face look bitter. "He whacked me around some and his friends helped him do it. I'm better now, but I've spent a lot of my days black and blue and hurting bad all over. They caught me and almost beat me to death. And then I got sent to Tepsicon because he had police friends."

"You'll likely be safe enough working here. I'll let you take care of the beach-side rooms just as soon as I've taught you what to do and how to do it. That way this bad man or his friends aren't likely to see you if they ride or drive past on the highway. And if any law comes by looking for a runaway from Tepsicon I won't say a word about you. But it's a good thing you told me the truth."

"Thank you," Jane Doe said. She smiled at Angela Cart and hoped she'd found a friend.

In a short time Jane Doe became a competent motel maid. She quickly learned much about the motel business. In a pinch she could fill in behind the check-in desk, accepting arrivals and departures and even answering the phone and making future reservations. She could fix a leaking toilet, change light bulbs, silence a drunken guest, or calm an unruly child. She soon found she could do all those things efficiently and usually without making the guests angry. She was large and commanding and people just naturally did what she said.

It remained hard for her to remember anything more than her recent past, but she had no trouble learning the new things she needed to do in her motel job. That pleased her and her boss, Angela Cart.

Now and again there came frightening nightmares when she slept alone in her nearby rented room. The bad dreams were about rough hands that held her tightly while crazy-acting men assaulted her in different nasty ways. She taught herself to wake up quickly from such bad dreams and then to think good things about her new and present world, a brand new world for her where the sea and earth winds were always gentle and she could be at peace with all.

After a few weeks she became restless, wanting to move on in her hunt for something or someone unknown. But she was happier, much happier, now that she was free. So she stayed on and worked hard. Someday she'd have to run, but not yet.

A day came when she again saw the man she'd seen before on the motorcycle, the one who'd watched and then motioned to her from the road outside Tepsicon. She also thought that he might have been one of the ones who'd done the bad things that had injured her head and put and then kept her in the asylum. She was sure he'd been some part of that crowd. But there'd also been a man then who'd tried to help her. Someone.

On this day, the searcher had likely parked his motorcycle

in a public lot up the sand and was walking the beach. She saw him when he was about a hundred feet away from the motel room she was servicing. He was looking at the building, and she thought it possible he might have been looking for her before or had caught a glimpse of her and returned for a closer look. He had a beard, but he also seemed very young.

She was panic-stricken and ran into the hall and then abruptly stopped, calming herself. She found she was suddenly more angry than afraid because this young man was hunting her. He was bigger than she was and she still had flashes of memory about the great strength of her attackers, but now she wanted badly to damage this man when he wasn't backed up or surrounded by a mob of his half-remembered shadow helpers.

Today she believed he was alone.

There was a bottle of Drano in her cleaning cart. She opened the cap and poured some of it into her wash pan. She knew it could burn human flesh like the devil's own hellfire.

She waited behind a door that opened to the outside sand walk and the nearby ocean. He came boldly through it and she threw the Drano at his face, aiming for his eyes. He ducked and missed most of it, but the burn and shock of it on exposed skin made him scream and turn quickly away.

"Stop following after me, you mean-ass son of a bitch mob boss," she said in a loud voice. "If I see you stalking me again, I'll do my best to hurt you bad like I remember those damned people hurt me."

She said it to his back because he was already back through the corridor exit door, running away full tilt. He was screaming something, but she couldn't make out his words.

Maybe it was, "Not me . . . not me." And then was it "Mom"?

But it had been him and/or at least his friends. Her head hurt with the vague memories. Suddenly she was no longer sure.

She decided it was time to move on, anyway. And maybe seek no more motel jobs.

She said a tearful farewell to Angela Cart, promising to write and, one day, return to visit.

She moved on down the Gulf coast by bus, clutching her almost empty suitcase close to her like a lifeline.

She found that the farther she got from Tepsicon, the more confident and less nervous she became.

Farther south the weather grew a bit warmer and it stayed that way. There were more people, and it was easy quickly to obtain a job. Potential employers would take her application and accept Ginger Cotner's social security number and seem to remain satisfied. If an employer questioned her too much at a newfound job, she'd move on. She was always able to find something. She therefore looked for places that seemed safe, not motels where someone driving by or a group of men riding motorcycles could spot and maybe trap her.

A job inside a building where customers couldn't see her was safer and better.

She cashed her paychecks and kept the proceeds in her suitcase. And she lived.

In Saint Pete, she found a job in the kitchen of a chain shrimp and fish restaurant. At first she was just the dishwasher, feeding the machine-cleaned results into a hot sterilizer, then removing the dishes and stacking them in orderly fashion on big trays.

A day came when a sometimes drunken assistant cook didn't show up and she allowed herself to be drafted into that job. She was all right at it and so, for a while, the restaurant paid her more money and she worked better hours doing her new job. One day the cook became ill and she used her meager learned knowledge of that job, gained from closely watching and remembering, and became the cook. That job was far harder and much more complicated. The manager soon saw problems and switched her back to assistant cook.

Soon she moved on, when she was questioned. This time she took a bus south to Sarasota and found a better cooking assistant's job out on Siesta Key, one of the several islands near Sarasota. It lay close to the city but had shorn away from the mainland by a long-ago huge hurricane. The key was covered with fluffy white-sand beaches, fine houses, large villas, and condos. There were thousands of affluent, indolent inhabitants, transients and permanents. The crowds waxed and waned with the weather, dwindling now as summer approached.

There was idle time to fill when she was off from work. She could sit in the sun at such times and enjoy the warmth. She liked that, and she liked walking the sands in neighborhoods composed mainly of huge hotel-motels, luxury high-rise and low-rise condos, and neat villas that bordered the cool, fine seas of the Gulf of Mexico.

She knew she was looking and watching and waiting for someone who she hoped was also looking for her. She day and night dreamed a lot about that.

It had to be someone who would not be riding a motorcycle. She was sure of that much. Her man had no damned cycle. She knew somehow she was looking for someone who was gentle. She hoped and believed this someone was also seeking and would recognize her. She hoped she would also recognize him but had no faith in it.

Something inside her head made her feel things had to be that way.

But no one came. At least not yet. She wandered and wandered the soft beach for hours, hoping for discovery but finding no one.

She made a few friends among her coworkers, and once a smiley, talkative man who delivered things to the restaurant where she worked approached her and asked her out on a dinner date. She declined, but she liked being asked. She wasn't sure she'd always say no. She dreamed about men, mostly a certain man, but she could never find his face or figure in her dreams. That was frustrating.

She spent much of her extra time in libraries. She loved the newspapers and map books and the quiet of libraries. The things she read in library reading rooms made her realize again how large the world was and how many people there were in it. Thousands and millions of people.

There came a day when she sat reading and intermixing the words she read with daydreaming. Something she read would set her off and she'd then sit with the book in her lap, lost in her fancies.

She became aware she was herself being watched. There were two watchers, a man and a woman. Both of them were younger than she was. They watched her for a long time, and now and then they conferred together.

She thought they were talking about her.

Not only did they watch, but they then fell in behind her when she left the library and followed as she walked toward her rented, lonely room.

She stopped near her door.

"Why are you following me?" she asked. Somehow she wasn't afraid of them. Their following had not set off any inner panic alarms. She knew instinctively they weren't working for any motorcycle man and/or his army of darkness. They were well dressed and seemed not to be problem people. And she knew inside her head that someone or several someones had to be seeking her, so all this could be a natural happening.

The woman, who was pretty, smiled reassuringly and nodded nicely at her but waited for the man to speak. He seemed to be in charge.

"Will you tell us your name, please?" the man asked politely enough. "And please don't be afraid of us. We're not following you to harm you."

She used the name she'd stolen at Tepsicon. No one had ever questioned it. "My name is Ginger Cotner."

"No, that isn't true," the man said, smiling easily, not upset by her lie. "But we think you do have her papers."

"Are you here to return me to Tepsicon Hospital? If you are, I don't want to go back there and I'll tell you now I will run from there again or run from you now if I can."

"No ma'am," the man said. "You won't ever have to go back to Tepsicon, although you had and have an attendant friend named Alma Dagley Jones there who told us some good things about you. She made you sound as if you wore shining armor when you were her patient and friend there. We talked to her a long time at the hospital. We'll tell you she's fine and her kids are also fine. She told us to tell you she missed you but that she was glad you were gone now that we were looking for you. We also talked to the doctor who is chief of staff there. In the hospital you were called Jane Doe, but we know your true name is Martha Cannert. Ginger Cotner, whose papers you carry, is still a patient at Tepsicon and we're told she'll likely always be there. Alma thought you might be using Ginger's name. She told us that. We know you came to Florida from Chicago. Do you remember Chicago? We went to that city and found out other things about you and your husband."

"My husband? How do I know what you say is true?"

"You know it."

"Why are you investigating me?"

"Do you remember anything at all about a man whose name is Charles Cannert?" the man asked, not answering her questions except with ones of his own.

She shook her head quickly and felt a wave of pain and dizziness.

"Try to think about the name Charles Cannert for just a moment or two, please. Try to remember him. You were married for more than thirty years to this Charles Cannert, and we think he's down here in Florida and has been here looking for you in many places. We also know from our own investigation that you were injured badly by people who attacked you here in Florida. You lost your memory or at least most of it because of those injuries. Losing your memory has made it hard for you to find Charles Cannert now that you've gotten better."

She listened to the words but then shook her head again. It hurt in her head to listen and try to think at the same time.

"What you say doesn't mean much to me," she said. She shook her aching head again, and then the words she'd heard began to mean a little. Charles Cannert. Maybe he was the man she remembered beside her in the shadow car she'd imagined was hers when watching the road near Tepsicon. A man. No face, but she did remember small kindnesses.

A good and gentle man, but strong, very strong.

"I maybe recall a little," she said. "Please tell me more. And tell me how you found me and how you know now I was or am married to this man."

"I have some pictures we borrowed up in Chicago from your and his old friends and neighbors there. Would you like to see them?"

"Oh, yes. Please, please, yes." She took the pictures in hands that trembled badly. She recognized herself vaguely in the pictures but knew no one else at first glance.

She had been heavier. She liked her new look better than her old one. She wondered if that was normal. Was she now some kind of crazy person?

She focused hard on the man in most of the pictures and suddenly realized she had seen and known him before. It had been in another time and at another place. That lost world seemed all vanished away from her now except in the small pictures she held tightly in her hands and examined.

The man was about her height, maybe an inch or two taller, not heavy but not thin. He had a good face, not handsome but also not ugly. She saw that his picture eyes were clear and he seemed to meet the world straight on with them. She liked what she saw in the pictures, and then she felt that liking grow inside her as she remembered some more things about him. The memories came slowly, but they were good. She remembered a kind and patient man who smiled a lot and laughed when small and even large things went wrong around them. He'd not talked a lot, but when he did talk it had been good.

She remembered loving him. That had also been good.

She nodded to herself, now more certain.

I will surely find you now, Charles Cannert.

The man's voice brought her back to the present. "I'm a police officer from Centralia, a small town north of here in the Florida panhandle. This lady, her name is Barbara, is assisting me. So that you will know about it and not wonder, I'll also tell you we hope and plan to get married soon." The man smiled at the woman, who returned the smile. "More of interest to you than us is that your husband came to my city some months ago. I met him just once and I think he was suffering from a bad illness then. While he was there in Centralia, a very dangerous man who had been harming many older people disappeared and has never been located. We think, make that *I* think, your husband knows something about what happened to that bad man."

"Is this Charles Cannert you call my husband in some kind of police troubles? Is that it?"

"I can't tell you for dead certain that he's completely without legal problems, but I'm mostly looking for him to ask him some questions about the bad man who vanished. I made a rough drawing of your husband after I met him in Centralia. By luck someone I showed the drawing to gave me a name and thought he might be the man I was looking for. There may be other police here and other places who are also looking for your man, Charles Cannert. I can only promise you I won't arrest him when I find him, although I hold an arrest warrant for him. I mostly want and need some answers to questions. I guess you could say I'm pretty much on his side because I didn't like and the police department I work with didn't like this bad man who vanished. I think and other police think this bad man killed a lot of people and that he likely tried to kill your husband, Charles Cannert."

"And the people in Chicago. Are they looking for him?"

"I can assure you that they're not. Do you remember a policeman named Inspector Steve Compton? Or a man named Jimmie Webb, who may have been your landlord?"

"No." Martha Cannert thought suddenly about her own situation. Someplace out in the world a man on a motorcycle and his friends who'd hurt her months back were still likely looking for her to hurt her more.

She said, "I don't remember much about him just yet except that he was a good man. I remember he'd been in a war or wars and was in the military for a time." She thought for a moment, not wanting to say much. "He had some medals, rows of them."

"Was he an officer?"

"I don't know. Maybe." She shook her head, remembering more. "No, he wasn't an officer. He was a sergeant, I think maybe a master sergeant. He was still in the service when I met him. He was sick in a hospital then, before we got married." She remembered more. "He had some wound scars and he'd been hurt and was also maybe sick with something like malaria or another fever thing." She nodded, almost to herself. "I worked as an attendant of some kind in that hospital and I met him first because of my job. They thought he might die then. And just now I'm remembering I left and came to Florida because he'd gotten sick again."

"I see. Did your husband have any special physical or mental gifts?"

"He was very strong and quick for his size. And sometimes he knew things about people. He could read them." She thought some more. "And he could see real good in the dark."

"That's good. What else can you remember?"

She thought some more about her own situation and forgot his question. "So you looked for me because you couldn't find my husband. How does finding me help you?"

"We're certain he's also looking for you and has been looking for you a long time. People who knew him and also you as a couple told us he has some form of cancer and might be very ill with it by now. You got lost and were put in a mental hospital and he got out of a Chicago hospital and came down here to find you. We intend to tell newspapers about our locating you. He will maybe read the stories about that and then come to us. Before anyone questions him about things he might have done, we'll be getting him a lawyer."

"The man or men who did me harm and put me in the mental hospital might also read the news stories."

"Yes. That's possible. We promise to protect you and, when your story spreads through the news, so will other police."

She remembered something else. "You think my husband is now very sick? I remember that he was sick and had been operated on when I last saw him."

"We think he has some kind of cancer, but we're not sure how bad off he is now," the policeman said. "His doctors up there didn't talk to me. I got most of my info from men your husband had known like Steve Compton, a police officer, and Major Jimmie Webb, men from Chicago who liked your husband a lot."

"Yes," she said, remembering some more. "Cancer was what he had." She nodded. "They gave him a year on the long side. I came looking for a place for us to be together, a place where I could care for him because they said he was terminal. Then bad people got me and I wound up in Tepsicon and it all got lost."

"Help us find him now," the man said. "We think he's likely still alive. Maybe even still strong."

"All right. I guess I want to find him more than you do."

"Yes," the policeman answered. "Now we'll look together. You can tell him anything I've said and I will answer any question he asks."

9

Teeing It Up

The golf club's ninety-plus private residences and its small lake shared a columned entrance that bore the sign SUN-SHINE LAKE GOLF ESTATES in weather-faded script. Underneath, it read, NO CHILDREN UNDER 18 UNACCOMPANIED BY ADULTS and, under that in even larger letters, NO PETS ALLOWED.

Cannert had read the golf club's want ad in a weekly newspaper of an inner south Florida town where he was now engaged in his dangerous game of hide-and-seek. He'd phoned the same day about the advertised job. His reason was not that his money was gone, but he'd figured it might not last out the rest of his days. The nursing home had taken a quarter of the funds that remained.

He was taking too damned long to die.

He had decided he no longer had complete faith in any

almighty being who overheard doctors' verdicts. Or perhaps that being had a faulty memory.

Before calling on a pay phone, he'd leafed again through his well-thumbed newspaper clippings and refound a news story he recalled about an earlier night of deadly fires with several Sunshine Lake houses heavily damaged, two area firefighters injured, and one unidentified female dead. That woman had never been identified in later news stories. Cannert was interested in her and most of all in discovering if she might be Martha Cannert, his vanished wife.

The fires and dead lady had likely been big news in the small town nearest the golf club and also a big enough story to make the metropolitan daily papers Cannert tried to keep up with. He'd managed keeping up even during the trying days when he'd been confined recently to a nasty nursing home.

His vanished wife was the reason Cannert had originally journeyed to Florida. Martha could have wandered this way, although the newspaper's brief description of the body of the dead female hadn't been promising. Too small in body. Martha had been, and he hoped still was, a large lady.

But there existed some chance Martha could have visited earlier or later than the night of the fires. That was enough to draw him. The golfing place was near Naples. Cannert had heard his wife talk favorably about Naples.

It was something to do and a place to go. He knew he was getting more sick. Sometimes he wanted just to stay in bed in the mornings and at naptime, but he still could get up.

On job interview day, Cannert arrived early in case there was competition for the job. Sunshine Lake Golf Estates appeared to be a good place for him to hide and look again for his Martha. He knew there were police looking for him, but he didn't know how wide the hunt was. He'd recently been close enough to a known police officer to spot the man first and not be seen himself. That happening had made him extra careful.

He hoped his searcher or searchers might overlook a small town like Sunshine City. Besides, life was a gamble he was certain eventually to lose.

Now, on this hot morning, he walked into the club grounds after a cab let him out at the entrance. It was a stifling day, but heat didn't bother Cannert. Cold did. Cancer, terminal cancer.

He lived on. Some days he did okay, other days he did badly. The most recent doctor had told him he could last longer in a hospital being treated with radiation and the latest popular chemo, but he'd ignored the advice.

Cannert knew a lot of things about death but not yet the final happening.

On this morning he was dressed in faded Levi's and an anonymous short-sleeved tan T-shirt.

The club smelled good. Cannert sniffed flowers and fruit trees. Greenery and hedges bordered the golf course and flowers and plants were being cultivated in gardens on the private member home estates that surrounded the golf links and lake. Many of the houses had their own backyard fruit trees, mostly grapefruit and oranges, so that the owners could choose and pick a fresh breakfast fruit.

Cannert liked fresh orange juice. Most food was something to force down, but orange juice tasted good.

He looked around again. The club had a look of faded neatness. It was, Cannert decided, a pretty place. Not huge money, but still expensive.

A few miles down the road lay a tiny village called Sunshine City. Beyond that was Interstate Highway 75.

Cannert believed what Florida novelist-activist John D. MacDonald had once written and Cannert had read, "Someone in charge of the place will one day asphalt the entire state of Florida."

He thought such was possible. There'd be condos with swimming pools for sale in the highway medians and also along the exits to the beaches. Big money but good living.

Yeah.

Life was better when you lived it warm. Such was what kept Florida booming.

Inside the club grounds Cannert found the pro shack. It was next to a much larger building that was parking for a fleet of golf carts. The pro shack was locked, but Cannert could look through windows and see things like racks of golf clubs and stands of confusing and complicated-looking machinery.

There was a fifteen- to twenty-pound black and brown terrier lying regally on a manicured putting green near the pro shack's front door. The dog seemed to be of mature or even late life years but not yet feeble.

"Hello, dog," Cannert said softly. He liked dogs and dogs liked him. He sometimes liked dogs better than the humans who claimed to own them, and he believed that if dogs lived as long as their owners, the dogs would be smarter when they got old. But dogs died young and that was a shame.

The dog gave him a lazy tail wag in greeting, stretched, and then shook his body. Cannert saw there were half a dozen golf balls nestled between his paws.

"Are those golf balls good to eat?" he asked the dog curiously. "Maybe I could try to eat one dipped in orange juice. And how did you get in here? The sign at the entrance said something about no pets."

The dog wagged his tail again and wriggled, offering quick friendship but no answer beyond a single polite woof.

"Tell me who uses that machinery inside the building and for what?" Cannert further asked.

The dog again had no answer, and so they waited and watched each other companionably for another while.

The golf pro eventually appeared. He was a tall man who had not aged well. His eyebrows looked like small white Christmas tree ornaments and his mouth was a combination of smile and distorted smile muscles. Up close he had the smell and appearance of a heavy drinker, but he moved fairly well with only a hint of a limp. His left hand seemed difficult to operate. Cannert thought it perhaps was affected by a stroke or severe arthritis. Cannert remembered the pro's name was Gordon Dickson from their phone conversation.

The golf man opened the lock of the pro shop door and clicked on a radio inside. He turned the dial until he found a station that played music. The music was mostly old-time, some of it religious, some of it pop. The volume was turned low and Cannert had to strain to hear it.

The pro hummed with the music and sometimes sang a word or a line. But mainly he examined Cannert and seemed to be deciding in his favor.

"You can call me Gordo if you take this job," the pro said to Cannert, smiling. He nodded at the terrier. "I see you've met my head groundskeeper. He belongs to the whole club, the only pet allowed. Plus no kids. They can visit, but only for a day or two."

"I saw the golf balls. Does your dog steal them from golfers?"

"No. His name is Tip and he's an honest Welsh terrier. He finds lost balls in the boonies and out of bounds or sometimes in the flower beds that border the course." He nodded and then continued, "Also he hunts balls down on Little Creek. It drains the lake into a river a mile away when there's a hard rain. He then totes the balls back here. He has no pride of ownership in them. I keep a bag of dog biscuits inside. He'll happily trade a ball for a biscuit. I provide the biscuits to the members free. They trade if they see a ball that might be their own. Finding and returning balls made a majority of the club members vote to keep Tip and so violate their own no-pet rule. There are no other pets, no cats, no parrots, and mostly no kids." He nodded once more. "Now, do you understand all that?"

Cannert nodded, but he was still a bit bewildered. He looked around for a long moment and then said, "I think I read something somewhere about some houses that burned around this golf course and a woman who died in the fire."

"Where'd you read that?" the pro asked, his voice suddenly cool.

"It was likely in Tampa or maybe over in Naples. That fire made news sometime back in the big newspapers. So I still remember reading about it."

Gordo Dickson nodded. His voice became a warning. "If you go to work here it's best not to talk much about that damned fire. It's still a hot issue here, pardon my pun. By now the area fire officials and police have mostly given up on it and decided it was likely accidental." He smiled down at his crippled hand. "I got this hand, which isn't as bad or good as it looks, fighting the fire that damned night. Doctors tell me I got overexcited and maybe had a small warning kind of stroke. Police are still trying to find out for certain who the dead woman was. They think now she was a prostitute over from maybe Miami or come up from Marco. They're not sure." He shook his head. "They do know she was dead drunk and died of smoke inhalation before the fire burned her to a crisp."

"Can I ask one thing about her?"

"Okay. But let's make it one thing only."

"About what size was this dead lady?"

"I read where the coroner said she was a small lady before she burned up. He guessed maybe a hundred pounds and no more than five foot one inch tall."

Not Cannert's lady. Martha was beautiful and tall. She also came with extra meat on her bones.

"Would you be ready to go to work today if I offered you the job?" the pro asked. "You were the only one who called

— 161 —

about it. I can use you if you really want the job and are over eighteen years of age."

"One more thing, please. What's the machinery used for in the other part of the pro shop away from where you rack the clubs?"

"You're nosy, mister. But truth is I work sometimes on clubs with the machines. I used to play on the big tour, and I learned about club crafting when I didn't make the cuts. I had lots of time for the learning 'cause I was a decent golfer but never a real champion or one of the gifted ones. Now, how about the job? I'll tell you first off it don't pay big bucks."

"That's not an unsolvable problem, Mr. Gordo Dickson. I don't eat a lot. I also don't have to have lots of money. If the job's mine, you tell me what you want done and I'll get right to doing it yet today."

The pro nodded, and Cannert, after filling out papers with fake facts, and doing some minor money dickering, had both a job and a new hidey-hole deep inside the machinery and golf club storage room. There was a bed, a toilet, and a shower all his own in one cozy corner. Cozy and so a good place to maybe die if that happened.

He moved in and went to work.

The work was easy enough. Most of the members of the club and the occasional nonmembers who drove over from the Naples area and paid greens fees to test the unremarkable eighteen-hole course were middle- and upper-class retired-to-Florida people who expected little and got just that.

Cannert cleaned clubs, shined golf shoes, and did both dirty and clean work on the course and in the pro shop. He kept the men's dressing and shower rooms clean. He watered course flowers and trimmed hedges. After strict notice from Gordo, he stayed completely away from the women's dressing room. The ladies of the club took care of their own dressing and shower rooms.

Gordo explained that to him. "It's damnably clean and it even smells good in there. It's not for rough, aging men like thee and me."

Cannert did mostly what Gordo Dickson needed or wanted. He quickly grew to like the old pro, who seemed no longer able or willing to play golf. The pro spent much of his work time playing bad guitar with his injured but usable hand. He sang sad songs about heroes from ancient times, poor wanderers, plus ballads about insane, lost, and murdered people. They were songs Cannert had never heard, but he liked them. Gordo soon admitted to him that he'd written many of the songs himself.

Sometimes Cannert would take out his own uke and play along with Gordo. He played better than Gordo but not a lot.

The two got along.

Gordo drank lots of wine and beer. He also willingly drank stronger spirits.

He was a gentle person and Cannert soon learned he injured no living creature on purpose. Sometimes Cannert would see Gordo carrying a spider out of the pro shop rather than just squashing it. Gordo shooed flies, bees, butterflies, and even wasps rather than swatting them.

Soon Cannert found he was running the pro shop most late afternoons while Gordo imbibed, sang his songs, and snoozed in an ancient, damaged golf cart that was set out of the way in the cart storage shed.

Because that seemed the way Gordo wanted it, Cannert also killed nothing purposely. That included members. He called the men sir and the women ma'am.

It was a quiet kind of job. Cannert smiled, said little, and spent unbusy times trying to teach Tip tricks that benefited the dog's biscuit holdings. He liked the dog a lot and the dog liked him in return.

Cannert also wandered the course with the dog when he felt up to it, which became less and less often. Wandering led him to the narrow, shallow river/creek and the long par-five eighteenth that lay on both sides of it. It was a hole members and guests cursed and despised, a golf ball eater.

Down the road from the club, close to the village of Sunshine City near the interstate, there was a 7-Eleven where you could buy necessities, including dog biscuits.

Some club members, male and female, were unusual. The most different and also the most difficult was a husky widower named Buzz Yanders. He lived in the biggest and best of the golf course homes. His house was almost a mansion with many bedrooms and baths and its own swimming pool. Cannert soon learned from member talk that Yanders's place was one of the several houses that had been damaged on the night of the fires. The still unidentified woman's dead body had been found in Yanders's burned-out front room. She'd been burned down to a lump. Some members whispered that maybe an accelerant might have been sprayed or poured on her to assure her death and destroy her identity. Yanders claimed not to have known the true name of the dead lady. No one could put them together before the night of the fire, but Yanders had admitted to the sheriff that he'd hired her by phone for romance and to upset some of his prim neighbors. He said he'd called her Tess and that was the only name he knew for her.

Unlike the other fire-destroyed houses, Yanders's house had been quickly rebuilt, with added space, more expensive than before. Yanders was, at maybe sixty-five years old, stronger in body than most of the golf world around him.

He was also overbearing, bad tempered, and a perpetual bully. He disliked the boys and girls from nearby Sunshine City who hung about on tourney days wanting to caddy for tips. He cursed such kids, the golf course, and all the world.

But Yanders liked Tip. The dog, in return, liked Yanders.

Soon, along with most of the club, Cannert disliked Yanders. He sensed that Yanders disliked him back. Yanders's only club friend seemed to be Tip, the aging, biscuit-eating club dog.

Yanders never requested things of others; he ordered them. Yet he treated the dog with a fine gentleness.

Gordo told Cannert a few tales. "Buzz Yanders pushes the other members around." He nodded. "He cheats when he plays golf. He tries to get older and lesser golfers to make bets against him, mostly penny ante, but not always cheap. He's got lots of earned or inherited bucks, but that doesn't stop him from wanting more, maybe all that the other members have."

"What else?"

"Sometimes he buys nice things for Tip. He seldom invites

anyone human to his place, but he charcoals steaks in the backyard of his mansion and gives the best meat to the dog."

"I've seen that from afar. I try, on the course, to keep the dog out of his way, but the dog likes and has no fear of him. Some people in the club whisper he might poison Tip sometime, so I watch him carefully."

"I don't think he'd ever hurt the dog," the pro said. "But he'd happily hurt any and all of the people who live here if he thought he'd not get caught."

"Could he have killed this visiting lady?"

"I don't know."

Cannert continued his watch. He observed Yanders playing the golf course during times Cannert spent cleaning and watering. Most times the dog followed Yanders. Sometimes he followed Cannert despite Yanders's calls and whistles.

Cannert liked those times.

Yanders removed obstacles to his swing and changed his lie when believing himself unseen. Yanders had a strong swing and could hit his golf ball a long way. He could also putt the eyes out of greens. He observed strict rules of golf when he played with other members who specified such rules, thinking to anger him. He forced them to do the same. And he knew golf rules.

His voice could be heard all over the course, quarreling with the world and other players, cursing the gods of golf, raising hell, throwing clubs wildly when his ball didn't do what he wanted and expected.

But Cannert, always on watch, never saw him mistreat Tip.

Cannert considered maybe doing Buzz Yanders in just for

fun and frivolity, then going on his way. But that would be unfair, even if it might be satisfying.

It had become going on time to move. No place was safe forever.

There was no longer a need to stay around. Martha wasn't here and had never been.

Cannert shook his head. He didn't allow himself to just kill people who were assholes. Doing hate killings was not part of the rules he'd adopted in Vietnam and now strictly followed.

He had to be angry and in fear for his life. And he had to know the adversary was also a killer, had killed, and would likely kill again.

Cannert's special favorites among the rest of club golfers were Damon and Katherine "Kate" Miller. They both smiled constantly and happily at the warm Florida sun. Their world included the dog Tip, Gordo, and Cannert as friends. Plus the rest of the club members, including Yanders.

Tip remained the only animal allowed inside. One couple tried to smuggle a cat into their Florida golfing home but got caught and were ordered to move or get rid of the cat.

They left huffily with the cat. Their place sold quickly and for big dollars.

"Rules are rules," Gordo said.

The Millers at times made Cannert believe that the "golden years" were real, at least for the fortunate few.

"I think they're maybe in their midsixties," Gordo told him.

"You don't have to tell your age or list it to join the club and they didn't. Bought their place three or four years back when both the Westlakes died in a car wreck on I-75."

Cannert watched the Millers and decided they were older than midsixties even though they camouflaged themselves well in perpetually fashionable golfing garb. They also drove a brightly painted golf cart with their names on its sides. They were the first to sign up for club tourneys and they were boon companions to all who lived in their golf club world. They sang merry, obscene songs together as they played the course. They joked a lot about alcohol, but Cannert, watching them, noted they drank sparingly and at times not at all. He observed that they were always touching and hugging each other affectionately. He decided they were still in love.

Cannert liked to pretend that the two of them were the same as him and a found and healthy Martha, living out the last of their time, bravely facing the end of life together in a fashionable golf cart, shooting pars, and bogies.

Sure.

And then, as he watched and sometimes envied the Millers, they upset him, Gordo, and all their golf club world when Damon began to play golf for money with Buzz Yanders. This behavior began just as Cannert was planning to move on.

And, of course, Damon Miller was losing to Yanders. Not yet big money, but good-sized dollars.

Cannert conferred worriedly concerning this with Gordo Dickson, who nodded and said seriously, "Aye, I've seen it also. Yanders will cheat them one way or another. He'll raise the stakes until he gets a chunk of their money." He shook his head and watched Cannert. "And that may not be a huge amount of money, Charlie. But there's no damned way I can interfere, good sir. Mr. Yanders runs this club more than I do. He's chairman of the golf committee and also on the club board of directors. He challenged me to a game once, but only after my arm got bunged up, a bit after I'd quit the competitive game because of my stroke."

"Can you play at all anymore?"

"Not even putt. I can, however, still teach and advise others. Damon Miller's not a bad player, but Yanders will likely continue to take him and therefore them, though."

"Would Damon Miller listen to you about improving his game?"

"Maybe." The pro smiled. "I can and will try."

"Would you allow me to work a clever trick on Yanders to help them?"

"Trickery? What kind of trickery are you thinking about, Charlie?" Gordo asked, smiling even more, liking the idea of cheating Yanders.

"I'm not yet certain." He eyed Tip, the sleeping dog. "Maybe something concerning lost golf balls and found dog biscuits. I've thought on it a bit but not worked out a good plan."

"Tell me what you can reveal now about this plan," Dickson said, still smiling but not as widely. "I know the Welsh dog has taken a fancy to you, but how can a dog like Tip help you and me and the good Millers?" He nodded. "Besides, the crazy pooch likes asshole Yanders as much as he likes you."

Cannert told him a bit or two more while Gordo strummed on his guitar, shaking his head all the while.

"Cheating him one time on the eighteenth hole or any other one hole won't get the job done," he said.

"I agree," Cannert said. "Not for Nassau bets or five and ten dollars lost on bingo, bango, bungo. But maybe if Yanders gets them hooked for big bucks, something might work out. Yes, a one-time cheat, only to turn the tables."

The pro shook his head, but he didn't say a word about interfering on Yanders's behalf.

Cannert watched Gordo instructing Damon at times during the days. Yanders also watched the intent lessons and grinned openly when Damon Miller blew a drive or missed a short putt. Cannert could see that Yanders wasn't worried.

Yanders hit the ball far and straight. Cannert decided Damon was meat and potatoes for Yanders, no matter what Gordo taught.

Cannert thought more on ways to cheat. He daydreamed about a situation wherein Tip, hearing a single, soft word of Cannert's command, would steal Buzz Yanders's fat billfold and snap savagely at the golf bully's throat.

By placing a dog biscuit in a prime spot, he got the dog to trade newly found balls for a newly purchased biscuit. But usually Tip wolfed the biscuit and then took the ball up in his mouth once more if no one stood ready to claim it.

The eighteenth hole was a tempting trap because it was a five-hundred-sixty-yard par-five from the men's tee. It was the only truly difficult hole on the course. Hit the ball long and straight to a narrow opening over the creek, then head back dogleg across the same creek toward the clubhouse. For a proficient golfer, that left a short iron onto the green, one putt for a birdie, two for a par.

Cannert dreamed about somehow stealing an eagle.

He'd not heard of anyone scoring an eagle during his time at the club. He asked Gordo, who shook his head. The pro said there'd been only a few and not a single one this year.

Cannert thought on trick balls that flew extra yards.

He also watched Buzz Yanders dealing with Tip and tried to understand the relationship. After a time he decided that Yanders, in his own way, loved the dog. He petted him, he fed him biscuits, he cooked special steaks for the dog to eat, and he never raised his voice.

Puzzling. He seemed to feel for the dog just as Cannert did.

Cannert decided finally he didn't want to make Tip into a villain even if he could make an illegal thing work. Tip would have to live on at the club after Cannert had gone.

He therefore stopped that part of his planning. It would have to be some other way. He looked around his world, seeking something else. And he thought of one other thing.

Then he learned, first from Gordo, and soon from others, that a match had been scheduled. End of the month, a little more than two weeks away, the last Sunday. Big money. Starting at a thousand a hole, doubles permitted if agreed between the two players. The word was also that Yanders had the Miller couple already several thousand in debt and that there'd been a few hard words between the good Millers and the bully.

Cannert decided for his own safety that he must leave soon and so he said to Gordo, "I'll likely be gone by match time. I've found a lost cousin up in Fort Myers. He's ailing and he needs me to move up there to his condo and help him."

It was a lie. He had no cousin in or near Fort Myers. To the best of his knowledge, he had no Florida relatives unless and until he found Martha.

He needed to begin that search again. He knew he was failing, becoming weaker.

Gordo didn't want Cannert to leave. "I hate to lose you, Charlie. But if you must go, have you thought of anything that might help the good Millers? I've been counting on you to do that."

Cannert sadly shook his head. "How good is Damon's game now?"

"He's a little better. If he's lucky and Yanders is unlucky, then he might win if all the breaks go his way."

Cannert shook his head. "Fools and their money."

"Aye," Gordo said.

He left late in the night before the match. That last night he kept Gordo Dickson company, drinking little (and pouring out most of his drinks onto the fine, soft grass of the practice putting green outside his quarters), with the old pro soon intoxicated.

Gordo played his guitar and Charlie joined in with his uke.

Cannert worked on for several hours after Gordo had passed out and lay sleeping in his cart, snoring from too much drink and maybe dreaming of his days of golf.

Cannert sneaked back into the grounds after the match had begun. He searched Yanders's vacant house but found nothing that was of help. Had he found a thing to indict and convict the bully of some secret murder, he'd brought along a rifle and a supersniper scope.

But there was, alas, nothing at all to find.

Cannert called long distance from a pay phone the next afternoon.

"How went the match, Gordo?"

"I didn't get to see all of it for I was suffering from a bad, bad hangover, but I know that Damon Miller beat Yanders handily by several holes and won more than twenty thousand dollars. I'm also informed that Yanders lost what little temper he possessed, threw his clubs against trees and later into the water, and swore off golf forever. He also openly cursed both Damon Miller and Damon's wife Kate. The good Millers have both said publicly since the match that he'll not get a chance to get even, not ever." He was silent for a long moment. "It became a most bitter match. Yanders had a bad-luck day and couldn't seem to hit or even putt the ball straight. Then, during the match, Yanders's only club supporter died."

"Who would that be?"

"Tip. We have a retired vet who's a member. He thought the dog got upset because Yanders was worked up. Tip had a fatal stroke or a heart attack right there on the course."

Cannert felt deep pain in his heart. Tip was dead.

"I'm sorry about Tip's death." He thought for a moment. "Do you have an opinion as to whether the rival golfers will ever play again?"

"Unlikely. The only person on Yanders's side was the dog. He followed behind Yanders faithfully, growling and snarling at other members. The rest of the club followed and cheered behind Damon Miller."

"Did you save Yanders's clubs?"

"Aye, I have them. I sent a town boy into the water despite Yanders's direct orders not to do so. The boy rescued them. They are now inside the pro shop and soon will dry out."

"When they're dry and when it's very late on this very night, put them on your machines and bend them back into true. Do that before Yanders changes his mind about not playing golf, which you know he will likely do."

Gordo was silent for a moment. Then he said, "You bent his clubs?"

"Of course I did. Some left, some right, some up, some down. Not a lot, but it seems it was enough."

"That's cause for a drink," Gordon Dickson said.

"Almost anything is, Gordo."

Gordo laughed.

"When and where will you bury Tip?"

By the side of the pro shop along with golf balls from all members. Tomorrow at noon."

"I will be there," Cannert promised.

The day after tomorrow was time enough to start the Martha hunt again.

First he'd shed a tear for Tip and touch the grave with a drop of his blood. He knew he'd caused the dog to die, and the dog had been a warrior.

- 10 -

Reunion

An over-the-road trucker stopped for Cannert near the junction of U.S. 41 and Florida State Road 92 in far southwest Florida. Cannert climbed inside gratefully, for traffic in this area was sparse. He was also tired and a little ill from traveling too much and too far. By now most of his life was spent traveling to places in Florida he'd not been to before. He still sought information about his vanished Martha but now expected little, even though the search remained the only true purpose in what remained of his life.

He was no longer holding up well. Sometimes he would be rackingly sick during the night, coughing a lot and with chest pain, but he almost always would be better when the sun rose and he could eat some food that gave his stomach something to work on for the day. Breakfast was his main meal and, at times, his only one.

Sometimes he became alarmed when he coughed blood.

The trucker looked him over and said after they were rolling again, "Don't see many hitchers along this road these days." His voice was questioning, and Cannert decided he was looking for a believable answer.

Cannert supplied one. "My Ford pickup died along I-75 late yesterday the other side of Naples," he said in friendly, soft tones. "They said they could fix it, but it's an older model and getting the parts and installing them will take a few days, maybe even a week. I got me this shack I rent off the road near the beach between here and Goodland. It's cheap and I'll sleep and then fish away the off time after I get to my place. I had to hitch because there's not many buses go this way and they want you to buy full fare." He held out a ten-dollar bill. "When we get close, I'd like you to just drop me off on the side of the road. It's not far now. It's worth this to me. And thank you for stopping. A lot of people won't anymore because I guess this is known as kind of a rough area."

The trucker accepted the ten and nodded, swallowing the story and now maybe feeling good about this whole samaritan kind of thing.

They relaxed together.

In about a dozen miles the truck driver came up behind two pickup trucks that were traveling together. It was the same pair Cannert had seen earlier when they'd passed and ignored him as he held up his thumb and tried to hitch a ride. Each of the pickup trucks had contained about half a dozen riders sitting or lying in the rear cargo beds.

The occupants hadn't looked quite right to Cannert and he was, as he'd always been, both a curious and watchful man.

The big truck slowed for a moment and then the driver blew his horn and passed the pickup trucks. Both pickups were displaying flashing right-turn signals.

The pickups continued traveling slowly along the highway. Soon, now well behind the big truck, both turned off onto the rutted sand. They were still within view of Cannert and the truck driver when they accomplished that.

It was a good place to stop for Cannert, but he waited half a mile farther so as not to cause questions or take a chance on being seen stopping by those in the two trucks.

This state road was only lightly populated with people and houses, but Cannert had heard when he checked around that a few people did live here. It was not far from the Ten Thousand Islands and Everglades Park. Some people he'd talked to had called it the ass end of Florida.

Cannert looked out into the darkness and then nodded at the driver. "Could you drop me now?"

"I ought to give you some change," the driver said. The two men grinned at each other as Cannert shook his head at the idea of change.

Cannert climbed down from the big but aging truck and waved the driver on. He stretched, not feeling completely right. Part of his problem was that he knew inside he should be dead by now or that he might die very soon. At this moment in time he still could move and walk. That was good.

Doctors had told him that he had only six months to a year

to live, and it was now past six months since they had opened him, looked inside, and closed him.

When the truck in which he'd been riding had vanished from sight, he walked back a way toward the pickups' exit point from the highway. He still wanted to find out about the pickups and their passengers.

Take a look.

He couldn't hear or see the Gulf waters from the highway where he was, but he could smell and sense the presence close by of old devil sea. This was a land of storms and hurricanes.

He'd thought when the pickups passed him earlier that some of the riders were prostrate and were maybe doing what might be obligatory prayers facing toward Mecca or somewhere else in that general direction. That had caught his attention. He'd looked for only an instant before turning away, not wanting to appear too curious, but he wondered about what he'd glimpsed.

He listened more as he stood later on the berm of the state road where the small trucks had exited. He could hear nothing except what seemed normal night sounds. There was no sound of truck engines, which meant the vehicles he'd seen had possibly now stopped somewhere.

The pickup trucks had left tire tracks in the mixed sand and weedy dry soil. The vehicles were now vanished into the land and closer to the sea.

There was a tiny sliver of moon in the black sky. It made enough light for Cannert to see. He'd always seen well in the dark. That had been useful years back in an old war and it remained a part of him now.

He walked with care and made almost no sound as he followed the sandy trail toward the sea. He hurt some and was suddenly short of breath and so he breathed deeply to help that.

Now and again he stopped and listened, but for a time there was nothing except the sea.

Then there was new sound. Something more than the sea, which he could now hear as the primary noise. He stopped and listened intently but could not make out what the fresh sound was or where exactly it emanated from. He moved farther on. He was as silent as a cat.

When he had drawn a little closer to the sound and the Gulf, he slid down onto the ground and crawled. Once some kind of large insect walked over his right hand, but he ignored it. It had been like that when he was in the tunnels. The bugs there had never bothered him much. It was as if they were his allies. The tunnels had taught him many things. He'd never lost the knowledge.

Ahead, he could now see what he believed might be the outline of the two pickups sticking up into the almost black sky. The trucks were parked near a sand hill and they were no longer occupied by passengers. Not being able to see the men in the trucks made Cannert more cautious. He moved on at half turtle speed. When he hurt, he rested for a while.

Soon he could hear the sounds of men mixed in with the booming and sloshing sounds of the sea breaking on and over the beach. The men were down near the ocean in a copse of small and stunted trees. They had spades and they were digging. Now and then he would hear words spoken, but the words were far away and in a foreign language that seemed somewhat familiar but not truly understandable to him. He thought he might have heard the language or one similar to it before but couldn't be sure.

Someone had started or renewed a fire that now burned low in a beach barrel. The extra light reflected against the sea. Cannert stayed where he was. He could see the men, but he believed they couldn't see him.

Cannert watched. He thought they were digging some kind of a hole in among the trees. Now and then they would dump the removed and piled sand from near the hole onto a tarpaulin with ropes attached. When the tarpaulin was high with the sand, a few of the men would drag it down to the beach and turn it over where the sea waves would wash the sand back into the Gulf.

He watched for what he knew was perhaps an hour. What he saw seemed to be the extent of it for the moment. He wondered at what they were trying to accomplish, but no answer came to mind. They were just digging a hole. But why were they doing it in the dark of night on what seemed to be a deserted beach?

Once all the men stopped and did a joint prostrate prayer session toward the faraway holy place. He believed the language he heard them speak came from a distant part of the world, maybe kin to Vietnam's hodgepodge of speech, maybe not. And he thought about 9/11. He would tell someone when he could. Soon.

Eventually, with care, he gave it up and moved away from the diggers and crawled back up to the trucks. There was nothing inside them to look over, and particularly nothing in them to bury or secrete in the hole.

Maybe they planned to return at a later time. They were doing something. There had to be a reason for the doing. So again, he would tell someone even if meant a chance for him to be caught.

He returned to the main road. Thinking more on what he'd witnessed, he still was clueless as to what they were doing. Maybe it was harmless, but he didn't believe it. He thought he might come back and take another look later to see if they prayed at other times and to try to recognize what it was they were digging or building before he took a chance with his freedom. Maybe it was time to think on coming in from the rain. He wanted warm food and a bath and sleep.

They were at the beginning of something, and he wanted to see what would be at the end of it. He thought some more. A chill ran down his back.

Cannert decided that first off, before food and bath, he wanted to find and sit in a library and catch up on the news of the world.

In a fine, cool library in Naples he read about Martha and saw her picture in a local paper. There were similar stories and pictures in both the Miami and Tampa dailies. He read everything he could find in the papers and then read all of the stories over again. He teared up a little a few times, but he smiled even more. The pictures showed a thinner Martha, but he recognized and knew that she was his Martha and that she was alive and seemed to be okay.

He'd almost given her up for dead, and his search for her had become mostly routine. Now someone had discovered her for him. The news story said she was in the Sarasota area on Siesta Key with a police officer named Sergeant Tom Ryan.

Cannert remembered a Lieutenant Tom Ryan from a town named Centralia up in the Florida panhandle. He wondered if that police officer and maybe others were setting a trap for him. He'd killed a man in Ryan's town, but that killing had been self-defense. He thought about that and mixed it with other things he'd done and believed a trap was both possible and likely.

He smiled inside and didn't really care. The trap would work. He'd help it work. Besides, he needed to tell someone about what he'd just seen on the night beach south of Naples. He needed to see Martha before the end, if it was coming.

Each of the newspaper stories reported that Martha was okay. She appeared very thin to him when he examined the news pictures closely. He wondered if some cruel captor had starved or perhaps tortured her. Maybe he had the strength enough left to do something about that.

Time to find out.

He took a bus north.

Cannert found a cell phone sales kiosk in a mammoth mall south of Sarasota and bought a cell phone there, faking the information he supplied the sales clerk and paying cash. He put the cell phone in one of his pants pockets.

To call about Martha for the first time, he used a pay phone among a grouping of phones in the same mall. He might need the cell phone in the future. The news story had supplied a phone number to call, along with several times mentioning Ryan's name and also the name Martha Cannert.

He had little change and so he called collect. A woman answered. Cannert knew the female who answered wasn't his Martha. The female accepted the call after he gave the operator his name.

"As I told the operator, my name really is Charles Cannert," he said. "I'm the Charles Cannert in the news story and I'm the man who is looking for his lost wife. Her name is Martha Cannert."

"Would you like to speak to Martha Cannert?" the woman asked, her voice eager. "She's right here in the room with me."

"Yes please, if I might."

There was a pause. "I'm supposed to have you talk to someone else first. Do you mind speaking for just a moment to Sergeant Tom Ryan so as to verify your identity? We've had some odd crank calls and some other attempted false contacts. There are some bad and maybe dangerous people out there who we believe are also looking for Martha. I believe your call is the one we and Martha have been hoping for, but would you talk to Ryan first? He's met you before if you really are Charlie Cannert."

Cannert thought about it. "I'm calling on a pay phone, as I'm certain you realize. I doubt you can trace me quickly should you be trying to do that in order to find and maybe arrest me. If I think you're doing that I might hang up and call again collect from another place or not call at all now that I know Martha's safe. But I guess I don't want to do that and I truly do want to talk to Martha Cannert. So yes, I'll talk to Ryan. We met a while back up in a panhandle town named Centralia. Tell him it's the man he thought was maybe sick, the one who bought him two scotch and waters."

In a few seconds Ryan came on the phone. "Your wife's here with me, and it's my lady friend who answered the phone. My lady's name is Barbara, and she's been using her vacation to help me look for your wife and then you. That's her only part in this. I got sent by my chief in Centralia to look for you and then talk to you if you want to talk to me. You can first talk to your wife, but I'll warn you that she may not remember all the things you might want her to recall. She wound up in a mental hospital for a time. Some people hurt her and used her badly. She's getting better and sharper every day, but she's lost some of her memory."

"I can see from her picture in the newspaper that she's also lost some weight. I thought you were a police lieutenant, Ryan," Cannert said.

"I'm not a lieutenant now. I'm a sergeant and I'm almost ready to retire. And I remember you told me you were a retired news reporter. I had to go all the way to Chicago to find you're not one," Ryan answered. "One other thing: A couple of your good friends in Chicago remain your good friends. They didn't tell me to say hello, but hello for the major and the inspector, anyway. Now, here's Martha."

The voice that came on the line was one he knew and remembered and for which he'd searched for six-plus months.

He'd not heard her voice for a long time, but it was the same. He bent over a little, feeling faint, but then recovered.

"Is that you, Charles?"

"Yes," he said. "I've been looking all over creation for you for what seems like forever."

"And I've also looked for you even though I didn't really remember you much for a while. I just knew I was looking for someone who knew and cared for me in another time and place. I walked away from a Florida state mental hospital when I got well enough to travel, and then Sergeant Tom and his nice lady love Barbara came with your picture and other old pictures of both of us at a party in Chicago. Can you come to where I am now?"

"Yes. I'll come as quick as I can get there and I'm not many miles away. Are these people holding you prisoner in any way? Are you under any kind of arrest? And are they giving you enough to eat? I'm not completely well and you don't look like I remember you."

"No and yes. I'm not being held a prisoner and I'm not under any kind of arrest. I'm also getting all I want to eat. I lost weight in the mental hospital and now I like being thinner. I don't think this police officer is really after you or has any desire to put you in jail. He told me he just needs and wants to talk with you, but he also said he won't let you answer any question that might get you into real trouble or even into minor legal trouble."

Cannert well remembered that Tom Ryan hadn't been a friend of the dead dog food boss man.

"He might not be telling you all the truth," he said, still

uncertain. "But I'm coming whether he is or not. I'm sick, but I don't believe it's contagious."

"I think this sergeant's a good person. He also said he won't bother you tonight and will just let the two of us talk."

"I don't want to have to go to jail if I don't have to. I likely will have to go sometime soon into a hospital again. There may not be a lot of time left. But I do okay some of the time," Cannert said. "It's been a little more than the six months and I still do pretty good most of the time."

"I'm real glad. I'll follow you to prison or a hospital if you have to go, but we'll hope and pray that's not the way it is," Martha said. "Sergeant Ryan knows about you being sick from cancer. He wrote out directions for me to read to you. So you listen and then come here as quick as you can."

"Yes. All right."

He listened to the directions Martha read him.

And in a little while he was there.

Cannert decided that both he and Martha had changed, and not all the changes were good. Maybe it was his own sickness, maybe it was also the fact that she'd lost a lot of her memory plus a substantial amount of her weight. She wasn't the same Martha. His illness and her incarceration in a mental institution had affected both of them. So had the separation.

Now they mostly watched each other rather than reaching out for each other. Before they'd been affectionate, always holding hands and patting each other; now they were reserved.

"How do you feel right now and how sick inside are you?" she kept asking him. "Do you have a fever? Are you coughing, spitting, or passing any blood?"

He nodded, not wanting to talk about himself.

She looked at him and made her own decision. "I think maybe you have a fever. Do you want something to eat or drink now? Food might be good for you if you have a fever and feel bad."

"How much do you remember about what happened to you?" he heard himself asking her over and over again. "You've lost a lot of weight. And who exactly were these people who held you prisoner and then hurt you? Tell me everything you can remember about them."

For several long hours Tom Ryan and his lady friend, Barbara, sat with them trying to smooth things along by saying soothing things. But, after a long while, that pair excused themselves.

"I'll talk to you just a little in the morning," Ryan said to Cannert. "There'll be a lawyer for you to discuss things with before I ask you any questions. And you don't have to answer any questions."

Ryan and Barbara left the room. The Cannerts were left alone to try to settle any problems between them.

Cannert thought it was decent of Ryan and his lady to withdraw. It made him realize he wasn't in any real trouble because of Dog Food Davisson's death. But he knew there were other problems.

The room the Cannerts were now occupying for discussion was the central room of a condo-type dwelling. It was nicely and brightly furnished. The condo had two baths and two bedrooms, one bedroom-bath off each side of the central room. The central room was composed of a kitchen and a big combination living room–dining room with windows. Through the windows you could hear and sometimes see a tiny bit of the Gulf of Mexico. There was a partly glass and partly screen door that led to a screened lanai. The condominium was on the fifth floor of a large beach building with maybe a hundred or more similar condos all inside an eight-story building. Charlie wondered if all of the condos had a view of the Gulf and figured they did not. You could sell the Gulf views for more than you could charge for a place where the sea couldn't be seen or heard. Cannert also knew that condos that looked out on a highway sold for less.

Charlie and Martha moved out to the lanai when things got loud between them, but it was overly warm out there. Charlie thought that was strange because the heat of the day hadn't bothered him as he'd traveled north to find and then see Martha, but now, on this confusing early evening, it did. Maybe he was suffering from a fever, but he wasn't sure it was that way.

They went back inside the air-conditioned condo. They sat on a comfortable couch. Sometimes they held hands, but mostly they did not and, instead, tried to understand each other.

It wasn't easy.

"I finally just walked out of the hospital in Chicago against medical advice," Cannert said, using care and picking each word he said. "I tried to find you from Chicago and couldn't, even though I was out of the hospital and had our apartment phone to use. No one we knew in Chicago had heard a word from you, and I'd only received one postcard from, I think, Lake City. I called people, police and the like. I called our friends in Chicago and I called places and police all over Florida and couldn't find out one single damned thing about you. You'd just vanished. So I finally came down to Florida to look for you."

"Feel my head," she said, moving closer to him on the sofa and bending over so that he could touch her easily. She liked his touch. It was as she remembered, very gentle. She liked that a lot.

He did feel her head several times. There was a large scar, but it seemed to be healed. Feeling the scar made him become angry at the world again.

"Who did that?" he asked angrily. "Who damn well did that?"

"I think some people caught me unawares and hit me there. That's my best guess. I remember some things about being held captive but not everything. They beat me and did many bad things to me. And I don't know what happened to my Plymouth. I remember men made me cook for them. They smacked me around a lot and tore up my clothes. Sometimes, when I could manage it, I hit them back. I still have bad dreams about that time. Sergeant Ryan now has local police guarding the building. He showed the guards police pictures of you so they'd know to let you get through to me."

"I'll be with you from now on all the time. I won't leave you alone and I won't go anywhere without you. You're safe now," Cannert said. "I think the sergeant wants me to go see a doctor soon, and I probably need to see one. I saw one up in his town of Centralia when I was there. I think he wants that doctor to look me over again." He shook his head, puzzled at what was going on. "He hasn't asked me any questions at all. It's like he doesn't care about what happened there in Centralia, like he just wants to forget the whole crazy thing."

"Did you hurt some people up there when you were looking for me?" She shook her head. "I know something happened there. I've seen you get angry at bad people before." She held up her hand to slow his reply. "Although it was always their fault. Was what you did in Centralia the reason those bad people came after me, caught me, and then hurt me?"

He had told her only sketchy bits about his life in Vietnam and nothing at all about later happenings. He had no intention of doing more truth telling. A story that was a tightly held secret inside him became nonsecret when others knew it. He knew that he loved Martha, but he realized he couldn't trust her not to retell anything he told her.

He shook his head. "I tell you once and for all that nothing I did down here or in Chicago had anything to do with the bad things that happened to you. I came searching for you because no one else could find you and people I talked to didn't seem interested. I'll add, just to ease your mind, that nothing you did down here or in Illinois caused any of my troubles in Florida."

"I think you must have done something you shouldn't have done somewhere," she said. "Otherwise why would Tom Ryan, a policeman from Florida, go to Chicago to ask questions and then try to find me in order to find you? Sergeant Ryan flew all the way to Chicago. He talked to an Inspector Steve Compton and a Major Jimmie Webb up there. I don't remember them, but the names sounded familiar to me when he said them. Do you, did we, know them?"

"Yes. I knew them. Both of us knew them. If you think about it hard you'll remember Major Webb. We went to a party at his home. And Inspector Compton came and talked to you after someone set off bombs at our apartment building."

She nodded, some vague memory of it returning. She remembered a little of the bombing and of hurting herself when she was blown from her bed.

"Did Ryan go to Chicago about me?" Cannert asked. Then he added, "Or maybe about us?"

"It had to be something that happened down here or maybe up there." Martha shook her head, not knowing enough. "I've thought on it and you must have done something that made them go to Chicago to find out more about you."

"I left the hospital in Chicago even after the doctors advised me I'd be better off not to leave. I drove to Florida to find you. I protected myself when a man in Centralia here in Florida tried to cook me into damned dog food biscuits. Centralia is where Sergeant Ryan was or is on the police force. This bad man was hot after old and sick people. He hunted them down and killed them to make food to be sold for animals. He tried to hunt me down, and all I did was protect myself." He thought for a moment. "You said yourself Sergeant Ryan wasn't looking to arrest me for anything."

She shook her head, trying to find something she could hold onto inside her, something that would always be right. She moved closer to him, giving up any hard questions for now. "Lord, I'm so glad to see you and find you again. It's that way even if there are still all these dark places inside my head. Will they go away?"

He kissed her soft lips and remembered them again. "I hope so and for me also." He shook his head. "I don't feel real good right now. Can we just sit here and hold hands and maybe kiss each other some more?"

"Where do you feel bad?"

"All over."

"We'll just sit nice and quiet." He could see her consider what was needed. "I think that some kissing would be just fine. Let's stop the questions and just try to be in this together as partners and married people."

"Good thought," he said.

"One more question," she said. "Are you staying with me here tonight?"

"I guess. But I know I badly need a shower."

She nodded. "Yes, you smell some."

And so he had his shower and they found each other anew. It was strange and odd but also exciting and it worked out all right for both of them.

They began life together again. But he knew she was still curious.

And he was suddenly, in the night, hungry. But he was almost always hungry or sick.

11

Martha, Martha, Martha

In the morning, Cannert was up before Martha awakened. He touched her lightly, but she turned her face away and began to snore gently and almost without sound. He remembered that she'd been a sound sleeper during the years of their marriage.

All had gone reasonably well after they retired to bed and so he smiled down at her and got out of bed carefully, now trying not to disturb her. He dressed quickly and quietly, noting that he would need to buy more clothes and soon.

He liked and had openly admired Martha's new figure, but he'd also liked her old one. He'd known other women before her, many of them in Vietnam long before meeting Martha, but they were now a pair, and he knew that for him it would always be that way. If the outrages she had suffered before going to the asylum had harmed her, he saw no trace left of it. She was warm and wanting and seemingly unharmed.

Finding her had been an unexpected miracle in his life, and he was grateful for it. Most of all now, he was grateful to Sergeant Tom Ryan. Ryan had made the reunion possible, and Cannert resolved to help him when and if it was possible. There were some things he could tell Ryan, but there were many happenings, particularly concerning child molesters, he'd better never reveal.

It was a matter of self-survival.

No one else seemed to be up yet in the condo, but when he opened the door to the lanai, he saw a fully dressed Ryan sitting on a metal chair reading a morning newspaper. He nodded and held part of it out to Cannert, but Cannert shook his head. What he'd wanted to read in the newspapers for a long time was now a reality. He still remained a pessimist, but he was, for the moment, a happy one.

The weather appeared to be fine. The early morning was bright with sunshine, and there was a light breeze from the Gulf. He could see a tiny patch of ocean water, and the sea, at least from the lanai, seemed calm.

From somewhere in their big condo building he heard faint music. It was Gershwin and he had liked Gershwin's music all his life. He could also faintly smell coffee brewing and bacon cooking in other condos.

He did not feel completely well, but he realized he was hungry.

He sat in another of the metal chairs, and the two men eyed each other in friendly fashion.

"Did things work out?" Ryan asked.

Cannert smiled a fraction. "I guess. I'm back in her good graces for the moment. She has a lot of questions, and I don't have answers for all of them and likely never will. Tell me what you can about the men or maybe the one particular bad man she says is or was after her. She mentioned him several times last night after you and your nice lady Barbara abandoned the living room to us."

"Later," Ryan said. He read Cannert's face and then continued. "The reason for no discussion of it now is we have guards watching things around this building and there's nothing to worry about." He shook his head. "Believe me when I say I think that your wife is safe and will continue to be. She likely has always been safe from this one guy she saw looking in at the mental hospital and who came looking for her after she walked away from Tepsicon and was working in a beach motel. We think he was her protector and not part of the wild mob that molested her. I've talked to him. He says they had a mother-son relationship and, after listening and questioning, I believe him. She cooked and washed for him and he gave her food and did his best to help her. He's also a bit short in the head. He's not a moron, but he's also not book smart."

"All right. Then I'll believe you. At least I'll believe you for right now. She still worries about the men who held her captive and beat and raped her."

"I'd hoped her worrying was over with you turning up," Ryan said.

"Not for her. She's got scars on her body and worse ones

— 195 —

inside her head. And her mind is vague and puzzled on just who did it."

Ryan nodded. "What happened to her from what we've learned is that groups of men and a few hard women now live off the sides of the interstate roads on useless land in various parts of Florida. They're pretty wild. It's mostly a thing where there are just too damned many people in Florida in the winter. This group captured her and made her work for them. When she didn't do as she was told, they beat her. The motorcyclist she's so afraid of likely saved her life and then took her to a hospital after the the attack. From there she was removed to a mental hospital and deposited there by the authorities. The state police didn't want what had happened to her getting into the news and scaring off the tourist trade. That's the way the Florida world operates. She might have died if this young man hadn't helped her. He is, once more, mildly retarded. He's age twenty-two but also big and strong. Basically he's a good kid."

"Okay, then," Cannert said. He thought for a moment. "So now I'm here and you've caught me. I saw you once when you were maybe out looking for me up around a bank machine complex up around Tampa and Saint Pete. How do you feel about catching up with me?"

"You're not my typical prisoner and you know it. Sometime I'll want to talk to you about where you saw me. Was that in Tampa or Saint Pete? I first asked my chief to let me go look for you because you came and questioned me in what was once a favorite bar. Your doing that made me curious. My curiosity deepened after I received the bag of dog food plus a dead man's driver's license. I mostly wondered how you got the best of Davisson." He shook his head. "But just for now I don't want you to say anything about anything. We'll work on your story so that both of us get it exactly straight before we tell what we agree on to others. I can give you one promise, and that is what happened in Centralia to Davisson won't be a problem."

"Thank you," Cannert said.

Ryan said, "However, moving on in this quasi investigation and exploration of your curious life, Charlie, later this morning you'll meet with a lawyer. That lawyer should be here, driving down from Centralia, in maybe an hour or so. You may be surprised by that lawyer. You can eat breakfast together. You'll meet alone, without me being present. However, I do want you to realize that the Centralia PD isn't the only police department that now has an interest in you. The state police and the feds also have questions. That happened after I began sending flyers out about you and, later, your wife. The good news is no one is in a great hurry to talk now that you're located and no one else has a hold on you. For at least the next few days, everyone is letting me have first shot. Again, the interest of these other agencies doesn't mean they suspect you of any crime. But they likely want to ask you about every unsolved crime that's happened in Florida over the last ten or twenty years."

Cannert shrugged. "I'll answer any questions that you, Sergeant, ask me that I can answer. I'll decide later whether I want to talk to others when you and I are finished. Right now I'd say I have some doubts about it."

"Then that's the way it will be. If they have questions, I'll let them give me their questions in writing and I'll cull them time-wise and ask a few that you can either answer or decline. Just now, to pass the time of day, and mostly because I heard a lot of interesting war stories about you in Chicago, would you mind telling me a bit about your experiences in Vietnam? What happened over there when you were in the army years ago likely isn't dangerous to you now in any way. It is, how-ever, very good background for me and will help me sell you to the feds and the state police when I discuss you with them. If what I hear now turns out to be a problem, I promise never to recall it."

Cannert reached into his pocket and found something there. He held it out. It was a small sheaf of papers, crumpled and dirty. "This is my will. I think that Martha will have lost her copy if she was carrying it. Could I ask you to make your-self a copy or copies of it, keep them someplace, and then give me my copy back?"

"All right."

"It spells out about shipping my ashes to Vietnam should I die. I want, when I die, to be cremated. My ashes, or part of them, then need to be sent to Vietnam."

Ryan nodded, seeing that Cannert was completely serious. "I promise."

"Were you in the service, Sergeant?" Cannert asked.

"I was. It was twenty-plus years after your Vietnam War was done. I never got sent overseas. I mostly spent my time as an MP. When active service time ran out, I didn't sign over into the reserves or join the guard, even though I was pushed and prodded. I never heard from the army after discharge. Maybe they lost my records or, more likely, just forgot me."

"They never forget," Cannert said, smiling a little. He looked down from the lanai and could see children gathering outside to play. They were excited and noisy. He liked that. He looked around some more to see if any suspicious adults were checking the kids over, but he saw only a few mother types hovering, watching, and guarding.

He knew almost all child molesters were male.

He hated child molesters almost as much as he loved the children.

"Whatever. You like children, don't you?"

"Yes."

"That's good."

The two men nodded at each other.

Cannert thought for a moment about where to start and how much to tell, and then began at the beginning. It was a story he'd told before to acquaintances and veterans' groups that wanted to hear it around Chicago. He'd been well-known around Chicago.

"I became an enlisted reservist in an Illinois National Guard outfit and remained one for a long time. For duty I'd go to meetings and drills in Chicago at a federal armory. After a few years they upped me to corporal because I'd been in longer than most of the other privates. Being in the guard, even as a private, paid a little money, and I could use the money. A part of the deal to be a corporal was that I train for and become a medic. That's what my battalion needed, and so I got ordered to take medical corps training after I got my corporal's stripes.

When I'd enlisted in the guard I was working construction and my guard outfit was an engineering group, so I was a potato peeler with a gun until someone decided I ought to be a medic.

"I spent guard time training and learning how to be a medic, and I liked it okay. For a time, before going to Nam, construction work around Chicago got slack and I took a job in a funeral home as a driver and general worker. After working for the funeral home for minimum wage, I found a better job with an emergency medical service company. We worked out of hospitals and did a lot of highway emergency runs. I mostly went high speed to car accidents. I spent my own extra money, if I had to, taking decent training given by experts, doctors, nurses, and emergency techs. I had a knack for it. I remained good with motors and things mechanical, so I also kept the emergency vehicles running for my guard group."

"And then you got shipped to Vietnam."

"Then my outfit was activated and my entire battalion along with other outfits were sent over when the war in Vietnam widened. All this was years before I met or knew Martha. I was single, I had no after–high school education or book smarts, but I was good with motors and machinery and could fix things. I also liked to read and study things and answer my own questions. When I became a corpsman, I thought about maybe going farther in school and becoming a registered nurse, but after I was discharged and after Vietnam, I never continued. But I did learn to fix people. In Nam the battalion got sent up into the hill country. The people who lived there were okay. They hated the North Vietnamese and the Cong far worse than we did. I had to learn to hate the Cong, but the hill people hated them from birth. The Cong liked to hit and then fade away into deep tunnels they built and constantly added to. Some of the hill people went in after them. It was dangerous, suicide work, because if they were caught they died, but still they went. Lots died. I got to know some of the hill people, and I became friendly with their monk priest. This Buddhist priest or monk thought it would be good if my outfit could or would assign a medic or medics to the tunnel troops. I felt adventurous and thought I could do it, and so I volunteered. After that I did it for a long time."

"Your Major Webb in Chicago told me you were damned good at it."

"Did he give you any reasons why?"

"He said a lot of it might have been because you had and maybe still have strong night vision."

"That's correct, but it was more than that. The way it is, I can see more than most people in the dark. What I don't see, I smell and hear. If there's any light at all, I can see. Most times when it was deep dark, the Cong couldn't see me. Inside the tunnels there's sometimes phosphorescence. I could see by it. I could also smell and hear the bastard Cong coming and going and then concentrate and guess on what was happening."

"The major said you were so good they gave you some medals. He told me you also saved some of your own outfit's asses after they got captured. Webb and his police friend named Compton were big on that. Big enough so they had me come to Chicago mostly to pressure me to help you."

"Martha said you went to Chicago."

"I did. I told them your problem in Centralia wasn't much."

Cannert shrugged almost unnoticeably. "Thanks for making it not much." He returned to the Vietnam War. "A lot of the time it was killing the Cong and treating the tribe people who got hurt in and around the tunnels. That's what I did. Saving a couple of officers from my outfit the Cong had taken prisoner was a one-time thing and pure luck. I saved a lot more hill tribe warriors than I did my own soldiers. The outfit didn't give me any medals for the tribe. On the men the Cong captured, they entered the tunnels with three of my officers as prisoners right where I was hiding and waiting. They would have questioned these prisoners and killed them inside. Afterward they'd have left body parts, eyes, ears, testicles, penises, scattered around to frighten those who saw and smelled them. The bastards were expert at both killing us and killing the hill people. They were ruthless about it. They'd usually exit into the open only when it was a moonless night. They'd wear or paint themselves all black and then shoot up the whole damn frigging world. As to me, I killed Cong inside and outside, but mostly inside. I was ruthless also. I learned, from the medical books and training, because I needed to know, where to stick a knife so that there wasn't any noise from the stickee. I kept learning things from the tough hill people and from observing the Cong and learning to use their equipment and weapons in my work." He smiled without any humor at all. "I killed lots of them so they couldn't kill me or us. My outfit liked that a lot, but not nearly as much as the hill people I worked with. I cut off Cong body parts and left them here and there also. And I mined and booby-trapped where it caused damage." He nodded. "The monk and I became close friends. He had some

English and I soon had some hill words. I became what the tunnels made me into. I believed in the monk's Buddha more than my childhood Christ."

"Who were these hill people?"

"The ones people heard and read mostly about were the Montagnards, but there were and still are a large number of tribes in the hills. They've warred with the rest of the world for ten thousand years and still are at war with the North Vietnamese. Vietnam has maybe two dozen or two hundred religions plus lots of people without any religion."

"I read something about that. We abandoned South Vietnam, but that didn't end all the fighting."

"It'll never end. While I was there the Cong poisoned our water and crops. They put out thousands of land mines and traps. They didn't care who got killed. And I didn't either. I stole the poison and put it where they watered. I moved the land mines."

"I see."

Cannert shook his head, now agitated. "No. You don't really see, Sergeant. I learned to deal with the enemies of the tribe by killing and then mutilating them. I became a part of the tribe. I learned their language and bits of their religion. Some of this religion was Buddhism, but it was also part ancestor and family worship. I became family with and to the tribe. I prayed when they prayed. I gonged gongs when and if that was part of it. I lived with their men in the tunnels and, now and then, out of them. I ate the tribe's food that they ate and drank the tribe's liquids they drank. I slept with some of their women when I understood it was accepted and a thing they wanted me to do. I believe, make that I know, I have children and now grandchildren there."

"All right, all right. Take it easy."

Cannert nodded. "Sorry, Sergeant. I get upset when I remember it. When I had to return home, the tribe and the religion still remained part of me, although I was very sick then, and I thought and all the others thought I'd die. I was one of the ones who didn't want to come back to the U.S.A. From what happened after I came to Florida to find Martha and from other things that I've done, parts of Vietnam and the tribe are still alive inside me."

Ryan held up a hand. "I don't want to hear anything about that and so I will forget what you just said. Your situation up in Centralia was that you killed a badass bastard who was trying to kill you. That's called self-defense in the state of Florida and in all other states in this country."

"I came to Centralia because of news stories I'd read about old people vanishing there and other things. I found a possible killer and stalked him," Cannert said. "I thought he might have killed Martha, and then he did brag to me about killing lots of other people."

"It might have been illegal when you were doing the stalking, but it became okay and legal when he tried to add you to his dead list."

"Okay." Cannert smiled and nodded his head. "There were others I killed both before and after the dog food man."

"Are you wanting to confess to something? Is that it?"

"Maybe sometime. But maybe not now."

"Forget any thought of confessing. Forget confessing to me

forever. Say no more. Okay, you returned and were put in a hospital. You met Martha there and later married. How much have you or did you tell her?"

"Bits and pieces." Cannert shook his head and smiled some more. "I didn't ever tell her a word about the blood, guts, and body parts. And I told her nothing about being a part of and living as a member of the tribe. I was in an army hospital for a long while and things got a little better. Being sick enough to die was how they made me leave Vietnam. I was bad off, out of my head. I was crazy. The tribe people loaded me up and brought me back. Martha then helped me get well. I loved her and she loved me, but I'd loved before. I told Martha what she wanted to hear about the medals but almost nothing else about all the other shit in my life. I know it's not good for me or for my life as a civilian to talk about killing lots of the Cong, but people in the outfit knew and still know. I worked hard after I got well and tried to live. Then someone tried to bomb my apartment building and Martha was hurt a little. And I got cancer." He shook his head.

"What do you know about the bombing? Your answer's for me only and I'll never say a word."

Charlie shook his head. "I don't even want to talk about that."

"Okay. I basically agree with your thinking on that thing also. Your decisions are right with me," Ryan said. "The world keeps changing around all of us. It's hard for our law, which is written down in thousands of casebooks and statute books and faithfully follows its old decisions, to change. I'm a policeman and I'm now about to retire. The rules I know and follow no longer mean what they once meant when I first was a young, bright-eyed policeman. And bad, bad people get better at being bad and at getting away with it. You can't give people who practice murder and terror all of the Bill of Rights."

"Were you a good police officer? I heard from some in the bar that you once were."

"I was. Then I got bored with the small-town politics and began to drink too much. That didn't help. So I became a thinker, a drinking thinker along with my local chief. Then, after I met Barbara a couple of months ago, I quit drinking. Maybe I'll be good at something again." He nodded. "A man has to do something to live."

Cannert nodded. They went back to silence for a time.

Later, while picking at eggs and biscuits in a restaurant near the condo, Charlie Cannert met with his lawyer-to-be.

She turned out to be a female attorney named Alice Burger. She was a fortyish woman with intelligent eyes and what he decided was a mean mouth.

"I'm Alice Burger," she said. "I practice law around Centralia, Florida. That's up in the wet and winter cold panhandle." She smiled. "Some people say you were in my town once and maybe, just maybe, had to protect yourself from a criminal bastard there who came after you and tried to kill you. So maybe we talk first about maybe suing the city of Centralia."

"Charlie Cannert," Cannert said, standing, smiling some, and holding out a hand to her.

Alice Burger shook his hand firmly and then gave Cannert a

small, plain card bearing her name, a post office box address in Centralia, and a telephone number in the same town.

"Sergeant Tom Ryan had me drive down here. A moment ago he pointed you out and then left me alone at the restaurant door. My first and likely my best advice to you is to answer no questions at all and supply anyone in authority your name only when they demand it." She seemed to think about what she'd said for a minute. "Maybe refuse to tell them your damn name no matter how mad they get about it. This Sergeant Ryan used to be a lieutenant, and he and the chief of the local police are buddies. I don't know the reason, but the chief knocked him back to sergeant. I guess he's okay, but it's a small and crooked town."

Cannert grinned some more and examined the card. "Do you have an office somewhere?"

She shook her head. "I'll tell you the whereabouts of my office if I think you have a need to know it. If any policeman asks for my address, supply him the post office box number in Centralia and the telephone number." She nodded surely. "And if you are thinking about answering any questions at all, tell them or him or her to first write the questions out containing a statement that you've been given no Miranda warnings. Then tell the officer that you don't want to give your answers to any questions without me being present."

"Who hired you?"

"I thought it was you who hired me. I got a thousand dollars in cash, ten pretty, pretty one-hundred-dollar bills. They were inside a blank envelope. I checked them out and at least they're not counterfeit. The sergeant said the money came from you. Is that right or wrong?"

"I didn't give the sergeant or anyone else any money to pay you. I do have some money both here and elsewhere and the sergeant may or may not know about that. Most of what I have with me is in the form of rands, South African gold pieces, one ounce each. Would you like to take a couple of those for a retainer and then maybe you give the hundred-dollar bills back to the sergeant?"

Burger shrugged and then nodded. "Okay with me. Or maybe keep the hundreds, but tell a different story about them from now on? Money doesn't come easy in cold Centralia."

Cannert smiled again and fetched out two Krugerrands from a pocket. "This pair are probably worth more than a thousand dollars what with gold prices being what they are." He found himself liking the lady lawyer and he mostly agreed with the few words of advice she'd given. He continued, "Sergeant Ryan also said that the state police and some federal people may want to ask questions of me. Do you know anything about that?"

"Not a damn thing, but my advice to you remains the frigging same. Don't even nod at them without me being present."

He examined her once more. She would never be a pretty woman, but she was striking. He had one of his usually infallible hunches that she'd likely be good in court in front of a jury, maybe his jury. Therefore he might need her.

"I saw something off the road south of Naples the other day," he offered. "Someone federal or state would likely be interested. And I want to tell about it or go back soon and look again myself."

"Save it for now. We don't need anything to trade yet. But

do tell me if you've done anything else in the state of Florida that the authorities could claim was a crime. I don't want to know what it was, but just whether you did anything."

Cannert nodded.

"Just one other thing?"

Cannert shook his head. "More," he said. "And what I saw off the road and on the beach might need to be told pretty damn quick."

"Okay. I'll take your word it's important. I'll make some arrangements."

12

Retribution of Sorts

A doctor whom Cannert remembered from having seen him as a patient months before came to Cannert's hospital room in Centralia and shook his hand. The doctor wore a rumpled suit, a loosened tie, and a tired look.

Cannert could smell the hospital around him. It was a smell he remembered well. He didn't like the smell. It was a combination of strong drugs, hard cleaning fluids, savage, repeated floor moppings, and spoiled and fresh foods. Plus death. Cannert had smelled death many times and so that part of the odor didn't bother him.

"My name is Dr. Allen Palmer. I hope you remember me. We first met several months ago. For today I'll be acting as your personal physician. I conducted none of your recent tests, but I did read the results. Is this procedure okay with you?"

"It's all right with me," Cannert said.

"As I said, I did read the results. Do you want to go through them with me now?"

"Can I have my wife come in here? And maybe my lawyer, Alice Burger?"

"Of course. That would be appropriate. Are they here in the hospital?"

"I think my wife's in the waiting room. They wouldn't let her stay last night in my room." Cannert wasn't upset about that decision because Martha still had questions and was asking them any time she found an opening.

"My wife will likely know where my lawyer is," he added.

In a few moments Martha appeared. She was guided by a crisp nurse in starched whites. Alice Burger came in behind them. It seemed very official.

I'm dead, Cannert thought, looking at the nurse who was frowning. He then inspected Alice Burger whom he'd never seen smile and who wasn't smiling now. *They're going to tell me now.*

The doctor cleared his throat. "First off, I will tell you, Mr. Cannert, that you are badly undernourished by at least thirty pounds. That's a lot for anyone your age or any age to be underweight. You are quite ill because of it and you must now begin to eat. Other than that you appear to be in reasonably decent health."

"How about the cancer?" Cannert asked, pushing it.

The doctor shrugged. "There's no sign of it being active now. We have some hospital people, particularly our diet people, who want to ask you a lot of questions about what you ate and did after I consulted with you outside this hospital months ago. They'd like to try to find out what's caused your cancer to go into remission. So would I. We know you didn't undergo any chemo. We also are almost certain you had no radiation treatments. Sergeant Ryan, our local police officer, told us you were mostly wandering around various parts of Florida searching for your lost wife and eating next to nothing. Nevertheless, you now are in remission." He shook his head and seemed puzzled. "I remember checking you over in the Centralia apartment you lived in months ago. You showed many signs of advanced cancer then. I believed after I examined you that you likely had, at best, half a year to a year left. Last night I reread my notes about seeing you, and after I read your new tests, I reread those notes again today. Cancer's certainly what I found then."

"That's what you told me at my apartment," Cannert said, nodding in agreement.

"I don't think my diagnosis at such time was wrong." The doctor spread his hands. "Now, for some reason, all signs of active cancer have vanished." He smiled and Charlie thought it was a good smile, very benign. "I've heard and read in a few clinical journals about spontaneous remissions happening but have never personally witnessed one. All your tests yesterday for cancer were negative." He reached out a hand and shook Cannert's hand again. "So begin to eat and enjoy your life, Charles Cannert. The cancer might flare or start up again. We'll hope it doesn't. Put on weight, but do it carefully. We'll have the dietary folks talk to you about what and how much to eat when they ask you questions about what you have recently consumed."

"Sometimes I cough up some blood," Cannert said.

The doctor shook his head, not interested at all. "Start with soft foods."

Cannert looked at Martha and discovered her eyes had tears instead of questions in them. Alice Burger had moved closer to his bed. She raised a fist in triumph. When she was close enough, she whispered, "Sue the doctor and the hospital."

He said nothing. Instead he pointed at his wife. "Martha, sweet, would you go find Sergeant Ryan and Barbara and bring them here so we can tell them about this."

A week-plus after his speedy discharge from the Centralia Hospital, Cannert and his wife were staying in the Town Motel at the edge of Centralia. He was not under arrest. He wasn't even under orders to remain in Centralia, but Centralia seemed to him as good a spot to stay as any. And Sergeant Ryan and his chief had requested him to stay.

There was a city sidewalk running in front of the motel, and Cannert liked to walk in the neighborhood both with and without Martha. The area was full of young marrieds and there were kids and dogs to admire and watch over.

He'd answered what he'd thought he should of the written state police questions, the ones Sergeant Tom Ryan had examined and then Alice Burger had further looked over. Many of the questions submitted had concerned offenses that had happened on dates when he'd still been a resident of the city of Chicago and the state of Illinois. None of the timely questions had much concerned him except one: "In the past six months, several men accused of and awaiting trials on child-molesting charges have disappeared from various areas in Florida and have not yet been located. Do you have any information concerning any of these men?" The question had listed eight names and also contained what Cannert knew or decided were their last known addresses.

He had lied and answered the question with a one-word answer: no.

Had he been hooked to a lie detector, he likely would have flunked five-eighths of the child molester question. He had known five of the eight missing men. Briefly. Two of the eight had owned Centralia addresses and were among the five total he'd been untruthful about.

The federal agents had apparently decided not to submit any written questions after they conferred with Sergeant Tom Ryan. Two of them had asked a few face-to-face questions concerning what he'd seen near U.S. 41 and Florida State Road 92. That pair had come to the motel room. One of them, the older one, was well dressed, affable, and obviously in charge. His name was Jerome Whitehead and he'd exhibited to Cannert an impressive wallet badge and identification card. He'd then asked questions. The second agent was nondescript and had scribbled in a notebook, perhaps writing down Cannert's answers. Sergeant Ryan had been present and Cannert had liked that. Now and then Ryan had winked at Cannert.

Ryan and Cannert had become friends.

"We're told you saw something that might be suspicious while you were traveling the Florida highways?" Whitehead had asked. "Maybe terrorists. Your lawyer told us it was okay to ask you about that and only that. We're following her directions and, by agreement among all parties, Sergeant Ryan is present representing the Centralia Police Department."

"It was some men riding in two pickup trucks, maybe a dozen men in all," Cannert said. "Ask what you will and I'll answer as best I can."

"You told Sergeant Ryan that some of these riders were lying about in the pickup truck beds and doing something you thought might be praying?" Whitehead asked. "Was that it?"

"Yes. I thought their prayers might be directed toward Mecca."

"Afterward, you instructed this over-the-road truck driver you were hitching with to drop you off down the highway and you walked back to where you thought the trucks had vanished and followed their tire tracks in the moonless darkness to near the Gulf shore?"

Cannert had nodded and said, "Yes, sir. There was a tiny sliver of moon, but the sky was a bit cloudy. That was the way of it."

"And you believe you weren't seen?"

"No one saw or heard me," Cannert said surely.

"Do you think you could direct us to this place?"

"Yes, sir. Or go there with you, if you'd prefer."

Whitehead, federal man, shook his head. "It's likely another nothing. We check out dozens of sightings. Lots of Mexes around. They ride in pickup trucks day and night and everywhere. They drink a lot of alcohol and pray a lot. Most of them are Catholics, you know. If we can't locate the place you saw, we'll come back and request that you accompany us."

Cannert nodded. He gave them specific directions, answering every question. It didn't take much time.

Since the single interview he'd heard nothing more about the pair of pickup trucks or their occupants.

Sergeant Ryan called and, with Barbara, came to visit the Cannerts' motel room. The two women, who'd become shopping friends, left for a mall. Barbara and Sergeant Ryan had set a date to marry and invited Cannert and Martha.

Ryan had brought hot coffee in a large, plastic container. The two men sat at the room's tiny table, shared the bad coffee, and talked after the women had departed.

"The federal boys, there are seven of them, are going today to try to find the place along the beach you told them about," Ryan said.

Cannert nodded. "I wondered if they were going to do that. I'm glad they are."

"Confidentially, I don't think they really believed what I told them about your physical ability to see well in the dark," Ryan said.

"Yes," Cannert said.

Ryan continued, "But once I told all the various police departments about your military background and Vietnam history, they lost interest in trying to fit you into bloody things like past mass and single murders and the like. Decorated veterans don't fit perpetrator patterns."

"That's good to know. How about you, Sergeant? Do you

want or need me to answer any questions?" Cannert said. "And what's happening with my smart lawyer, Alice Burger?"

Ryan shrugged eloquently. Both men now recognized that he'd made Cannert into a hero. He no longer would or could blame Cannert for anything he'd done and now trusted him on all. Ryan said, "I don't want or need any more answers. You're safe with me. Alice Burger knows that. Miss Pruneface knows I'm visiting and she said to just tell you she had to be in court. When Alice believes a police officer is trustworthy, then that's a new day dawning in her profession. I'll listen to whatever you want to tell me. Same deal as before in that I'll not repeat what you tell me to anyone else unless you specifically agree to it. And, as before, I'm not giving you your Miranda warnings and so I can't be forced to testify or repeat what you say should some prosecutor get cute ideas. My chief more than agrees with this. He thinks you may be a gift from heaven. Is there something inside itching you?"

"Maybe a couple of things that might be of local help. When I first arrived in Florida, I stayed a few days up around Jacksonville. I set fire to a motel up there named Mom's Motel. I read in the papers later that the motel owners burned to death. The couple were in the joint business of poisoning guests for profit. They used some kind of strong poison. I thought the poison was maybe alkaline in nature when I poured it out. They'd then bury the body or bodies under the sand near their motel and sell or junk the leftover vehicles. The male owner, his name was Ed Bradford, had been a car salesman in the Northeast. They tried to poison me, but I got some sleeping tablets into Ed and his wife, Emma, when they were feeding me my intended farewell meal. I truly believed at the time they'd maybe gotten Martha."

"Okay. Near Jacksonville," Sergeant Ryan said, nodding. "I remember reading something in the newspapers about a motel fire. These people were killing their guests?"

"Yes. They'd been doing it for a while. I'd estimate they'd killed at least eight before I happened along. They needed the extra money to prosper in business. What I'm telling you might solve some disappearances."

Ryan nodded. "I understand. Thank you. Anything else?"

Cannert nodded. "I'm used to keeping all things I do to myself, but I'm going to trust you because you found Martha. I owe you and know it. So I'll tell you also about two Centralia gentlemen I did in over and above the dog food man. That will be it, at least for today. Maybe what I say can be of use to you and your good chief. The state police gave me the names of two Centralia men charged with child molesting who disappeared while on bond. They haven't been found. There were eight molesters listed altogether in the question. Two were from Centralia. Do you remember that from the long list of questions?"

"Sure. I know who those two were. We've been looking for them for several months. They failed to appear for court proceedings and their bonds were forfeited or are now in the process of being forfeited."

"I'll tell you only that you need not look for them anymore. They're not available to be found."

Ryan shrugged, liking it. "Okay. That's good to know. I know you did something to them that might have been somewhat illegal, so I'll not mention anything now. Sometime I'll pass the word we can stop looking. I'll never admit that the information came from you."

Cannert nodded and then, surprisingly, continued. "When I was searching for Martha and got to a town new to me, I'd go first to the library and look around. I did that when I arrived in the Centralia area. But before Centralia, I stayed nearby in another town. I read the back issues of their local newspaper. I found nothing there and so drove here and read your local newspaper. Your paper does a good job. They like to go backward into criminal case histories when it looks as if someone maybe got away with something. I mean like being found not guilty of child molestation, and then the same innocent defendant gets charged with a new molestation crime."

Ryan held up a hand. "You can stop there if you want. Those two had money and bought their way out of several things."

"I'll go a bit farther. One male molester was thin and the other was fat. That's how I remember them. Both were fiftyish. I followed the thin one and later the fat one. The thin one was warm on the trail of a small boy who looked to be maybe nine or ten years old, blondish, blue eyes. Your local thin nut was carrying a knife and some ropes with him. I knew his name from the news stories I'd read. He'd been accused of doing sex things to several boys before. A sharp lawyer, not Alice Burger, had gotten him off on the early charges. I thought he was going to do worse things to this newly stalked victim with the knife and ropes. Your other molester was the fat man. He was following a girl who was maybe eleven or twelve and just starting to blossom. Pretty girl. I saw her in a crowd of kids and observed he was following, let's call it stalking, her. I believed he likely was going to kill her, and maybe afterward, if he could work it, eat some bits of her. He'd bought some condiments in one of your local chain grocery stores. He had the spices and his equipment on his person and was carrying a cookbook also. I saw this. He never noticed me. So maybe, maybe not, a feast."

"And now both men are vanished."

"Yes," Cannert said. "Vanished is a good word. It fits what happened to the two men."

"I recall both of them had done jail and/or prison time and were heavily into counseling," Ryan said, shaking his head.

"Child molesters don't want to be other than what they are and don't learn from being caught or counseled. Many molesters get cured only by death. Only a few quit after getting caught."

"Maybe like those guys who bombed your apartment building in Chicago? Where your Martha got hurt?" Ryan asked, smiling.

"I don't know a thing about that," Cannert said, looking away, his face completely without expression. "Molesters who can't quit have an odor to them. Your two had that smell."

"Okay, I'll stop the police looking for the missing child molesters. But not yet?"

"I'd guess not yet. Sometime."

"Yeah. It wouldn't be smart to do it just now for another reason. I retire soon. Along with the chief. The city is going to give us a ceremony, a dinner, and a gold watch each. Chief Todd and I want to talk to you sometime soon about your future. We think you may be interested in this area's worst problem. Both of us together think that. We're also thinking of becoming private detectives. Would you like to maybe go in with us as a partner, stay around sunny Centralia?"

Cannert smiled and realized he at least liked being asked. "Maybe. It'd be something to do. Sometimes I don't really like doing what I've done the last few months. I try not to dwell on it anymore. I kind of had to do things when I looked for Martha. Now I've found Martha. Actually, you found her for me. I can now quit searching for someone who might have murdered her."

"How about molesters?"

"Most child molesters need to die," Cannert said. "Before we got too civilized, they did. Or they put them inside a prison or an asylum and never let them out."

"Yes. I agree with you on that. Many police do. And we've a problem in this area."

The men nodded at each other.

Ryan continued. "Chief Todd and I both approve of your extra hobby while you searched for your wife. You seem to have done more than what we've accomplished over most of our police lives." He shook his head. "I keep watch and I read things in the papers. So does Chief Todd. And our courts keep messing themselves up and getting things more and more confused. Our prisons are overfull. So are our jails. Guys who shouldn't be running free get left running free. The rich can buy or con themselves a bond. Only poor and dumb people don't make bond. Plus everything gets appealed." He nodded. "Think on it. We'll talk some more. How are you on money?

Todd and I have some we got up front when we informed area groups about our retirement plans."

"I'm okay," Cannert said. "Better than okay. I've got some assets you don't know about." He smiled and then the two said no more.

The next day Ryan brought a young man to visit Martha and Charlie. He was cleanly shaved and a shade away from handsome. He shook hands with Cannert but didn't seem completely comfortable in it. He had a limp that was almost indiscernible.

Martha was out walking. She'd made some friends in the neighborhood.

"This is Paul Langston," Ryan said. "He's the one who delivered Martha to a hospital after rescuing her from a bad mob. The mob was mostly crazies camping just off one of the interstate rest stops some months back. He's also the one who looked for her after she walked at Tepsicon. When he caught up with her, she tried to drown him in Drano."

"I'm sorry," Langston said, his face turned away. "I done it dumb and wrong and I guess I sorta scared her." He put out his hand to shake again and Cannert shook it.

"Paul knows he's not a rocket scientist, but he has a job working on motorcycles and he's good at it. His main hobby is helping people," Ryan said softly. "I'll vouch for the fact he's good at both things. Would you want him to remeet Martha today? It might be time."

Cannert thought about it. "That would be okay. She's better

in her head and remembers more now. She went for a short walk. She has a dozen friends in the neighborhood. We'll be careful about how we do it."

"The sergeant made me shave my beard," Langston said. "I liked my beard." He became silent.

The three men talked about the weather and other minor things until Martha came back.

"It's fine outside," she said and then stopped talking, seeing a face she didn't recognize.

"Martha," Ryan said, "do you remember this young man?"

"He saved your life," Cannert added quickly.

Martha shook her head and then smiled, surprising all three of the men. "I remember now. You were the one I thought of as my son." She touched his face. "You got me food and helped me. I remember you now." She smiled some more. "You also make me think I must write to Angela Cart, who gave me a job." She patted the young man once more. "Are you hungry?" she asked.

And all was well.

There was another day when FBI men came in force, a dozen of them. That was after Charlie and Martha had bought a furnished double-wide at an estate sale and moved in. The place was in a subdivision of almost all double-wides, some of them very fancy. The one the Cannerts bought was comfortable. The subdivision had a heated pool and several shuffleboard areas plus one par-fifty-four eighteen-hole golf course. The Cannerts found themselves younger than some of the occupants but not all of them.

The FBI came in three cars. If they were armed, they weren't showing it.

Jerome Whitehead was the officer who knocked on the double-wide's door.

Cannert smilingly opened his door.

"We went to the place off the highway in far south Florida you told us about," Whitehead said. "We can't tell you whatall happened, but I brought a higher-up and a note. Can a few of us come in?"

Cannert nodded. Whitehead and two others entered.

Cannert thought he might have seen the oldest one of the visitors before. Maybe on television. Inside, he took charge.

He shook Cannert's hand. "My name is Andrew McNair. I'm a kind of liaison between the Homeland Security office and the FBI. Thank you for the information. What I'll tell you is private and not yet for publication. The people you saw digging on the beach planted some stuff that, if exploded, would have caused trouble. After we found it, we searched north and south of where it was hidden. There were other caches. I brought a short letter for you. You can read it but not keep it. Up the line it'll get rewritten and added to before being sent officially to you. There's also another similar letter for Sergeant Ryan. Is he here?"

"Not yet," Cannert said. "I can call him." He started for the phone. Halfway there, he heard Ryan's car.

"That's him," Cannert said.

McNair waited and then started again when Ryan was in the room.

"I already told Mr. Cannert there was a problem at the beach. The FBI chases so many false alarms. When we find something real, we don't always know how to treat it." He handed Cannert a letter on fine, thick stationery and then gave another letter to Sergeant Ryan.

"Read and then exchange these letters so both of you've read both letters. Then give them back to me. You'll get them formally plus more after this matter is completed."

Cannert read his. "Dear Charles Cannert: My personal, heartfelt thanks for your brave action." It was signed by someone whose name Cannert could not make out.

Andrew McNair saw him puzzling and said, "Homeland Security assistant chief. Nice man."

Cannert handed his letter to Sergeant Ryan and took Ryan's in return. Ryan's read: "Thank you for your help in thwarting a terrorist plot." It was signed by the same official.

Five minutes after the letters were back in the possession of Andrew McNair, all the FBI agents were gone.

Cannert and Ryan waited until they were certain the episode was finished and then had a joint laughing fit.

They held a planning meeting concerning the proposed private detective agency. Present were Charlie Cannert, Tom Ryan, Police Chief Albert Todd, and the attorney for the proposed corporation, Alice Burger.

Martha was not present. She was taking her savior son from before Tepsicon to lunch. He was her current project.

"I promise this is not some kind of business meant to get you and us into any trouble, Charlie," Chief Todd said. "We'll be working within and mostly with area law. It won't be what we've done before."

"He knows that," Ryan said. "I told him."

Chief Todd continued, "What it is, we had a really bad man who lived here in Centralia for a short time. He built a huge house out in the boondocks. It was a fortress. He claimed to be a minister of the gospel, a bishop or maybe an archbishop. He was, among other things, crazy about kids, but such was only a hobby. Likely it still is. He's now very old."

"If kids are his hobby, what's his occupation?" Cannert asked, interested.

Todd said, "It's legend that he, Arturo Romero, retired out of Cuba maybe around the time Castro took over. It might even be true. We checked him out when he came to Centralia. By that time, many years after Castro took charge, it was tough to find out what's real and what's not. For a time Romero was up around Boston. Then he operated out of Miami for a lot of years. It said in our report that he's worth a couple of billion dollars. That's not million but *billion*. We put what heat we could on him here in Centralia. He ignored us and sued us. At near the same time, the local sheriff's candidate he was backing with big bucks miraculously lost the election by a few hundred votes. Some of us helped fix that election. So he moved close by where things were easier and now lives in and runs our next-door county. Things there have gone well for him. He still preys on Centralia kids, but he preys on any and all kids. He's into drugs, importing and selling them. He runs his own church and he has many followers. He wears robes and he's now maybe eighty to ninety years old. He gives kids he likes or is smitten by anything they ask for."

"He operates a real church?"

"They mostly convert runaway kids, lots of them. They're pretty rigid," Ryan said. "It works. He's got some very smart people who work with him. If he died, those people would likely continue things."

Todd continued, "There's a Centralia citizen group that helps out and works with the police. They've got money, but not the kind of money Romero has. Such citizen groups are now common all over the country and very strong in our area of Florida. They'll pay us to get rid of him, either force him into another move or get rid of him some other way. That would be moving him out of this state, maybe out of the country." He smiled. "Maybe even out of the world."

"Are there lawyers and judges in your citizen groups?" Cannert asked.

"Many, many. Federal and state. Lots of them with good ideas that are hard to work into the lawbooks."

"Tell me more," Cannert said, interested. "What do we need first?"

"We could foremost use a place in his county, a secret place. We looked around and found a couple of places that would work. They adjoin each other. One's a ranch where absentee corporate owners raise cattle. It's in the other county but on the line with our county. The other's a crematory. It's owned by a corporation also."

"A ranch and a place where dead human bodies are cremated?" Cannert asked.

"We wrote to the corporation that owns both places but have not heard anything," Todd said, shaking his head.

Cannert smiled, but only a little. "Do you know the name and address of the corporation?"

Todd rustled through papers. "It's called Green River Company."

"Address?"

"Chicago, Illinois."

Cannert looked at Ryan. "Does that name remind you of something, Sergeant?"

Ryan looked puzzled.

"What was the name of the apartment building where Martha and I lived in Illinois? And how did I possibly get rid of multiple bodies both here and up in Chicago, or actually Milwaukee? And didn't I tell you that your local molesters were *vanished*?" He waited for a long, pregnant moment.

"Charlie?" Ryan said.

"Act respectful, Sergeant, the owner of all the stock in the Green River Corporation is now speaking," Cannert said. "I told you I stopped at your neighboring town before I came to Centralia."

"Jesus," Todd said.

"No, just old Charlie Cannert. I once bought and used a crematory on the outskirts of Milwaukee. I know crematories and how to operate them. I learned about them as a young man working for a funeral home. I don't know whether we can get rid of your neighbor or not, but we do have two useful places to start from."